THE REVENGEFUL CHILD OF DACHAU PRISON

WILLIAM H. BLAIR

WILLIAM H. BLAIR

CHAPTER 1

It's the mid-1970s on a summer evening that is a perfect night for sleeping. In San Diego this time of year, those are few and far between. David Adelman and his wife Loraine are sound asleep, as are their two children. One would think that all is well in the Adelman family. That is, until you look closely at David.

He is in the middle of a nightmare, the same nightmare he has been living with for most of his life. The sweat is pouring off him, completely saturating his T-shirt and even his shorts. Upon looking closely at his face, you can almost see the action taking place: his face grimaces as each event takes place and the horror of it begins to unfold.

Tossing and turning and sometimes even flailing his arms about, David has lived this dream hundreds if not thousands of times in his life. It ends the same way each time. He hears the screams in his head over and over, time after time, and realizes that there is nothing he can do to stop it. As the sweat builds, so do the emotions. He finally sits up in bed with his arms out stretched, yelling, "Stop! *Stop! Please stop!*"

As always, when he is home, his wife Loraine reaches over and grabs him. She hugs him as strongly as she can in an attempt to comfort him, while at the same time shaking him and telling him, "Wake up. Wake up, David Wake up, honey. Wake up."

In about three or four minutes, the ritual is over. I say ritual because they have been through this so many times in their lives, it almost seems like a rite of passage for David, for some reason.

As soon as reality begins to set in, the two of them start to talk. Loraine reminds David, "Honey, you do remember that this is the day we have talked about for so long? Remember last week, we decided that it was time for you to get some professional help with this problem? We agreed to do this, so I have made an appointment for you with Dr. Flarity. It's today at 2:00 PM in his office downtown."

She hugs her husband and says, "God, I hope he is able to give you some relief. If only we knew what the issue was that you are battling. If we knew that, then maybe we could face the issue. Honey, together we can beat anything—our family is strong. So please, keep an open mind when you meet with the doctor. I know how you feel about this, but it is important that we get some help to solve this problem. Remember, hon, we all love you, and your problem is our problem, as well."

David nods his agreement and then sits up on the edge of the bed, trying to compose himself.

As usual, the two of them go through the same ritual after one of David's nightmares. David has to shower and change his underclothes, which are saturated with sweat. Loraine changes the bed sheets and pillow cases. By the time they're done, it is time to get up, get the kids dressed, and put breakfast on the table.

That next morning, the entire family is sitting at the kitchen table finishing breakfast as David is about to head for the base.

Loraine reminds him, "2:00. Don't forget."

"Don't worry, hon, I won't forget," he says.

Out the door he goes, jumping into his Humvee, which is a modern version of the military jeep. The Navy supplies him this vehicle for his transportation. David is a really good looking man: six feet four inches tall and a solid 198 pounds without an ounce of fat on him anywhere. He is a lieutenant commander in the U.S. Navy and a team leader for one of the Navy's elite SEAL teams, SEAL Team number eight, to be exact.

He is stationed at Coronado Naval Station near San Diego, California.

David makes his usual drive to the base and parks in front of his office then begins his normal daily duties. He salutes the sailors who pass as he makes his way to his office, stopping from time to time to chat with friends and fellow warriors. He has come to know most of these men, and thinks of them as his military family. The bond between them is unique in the military.

The Navy SEALs are a very small organization, so you get to know each and every one of them. It goes without saying that you know them very intimately, as your life can depend upon it. Rank is always respected among the men but the individual person is the one who really gets the respect.

As David walks into the office, he is greeted by one of his team members, Petty Officer William Finnegan, or Finney, as the guys call him.

Finney is a southern boy and about as loyal as they come, especially to Commander Adelman. The two have developed a bond that will last a life time. He looks up and says, "Good morning, boss."

The guys in the team call David boss among themselves; it is meant as a term of respect. When out in the field, however, and in front of others, he is called "Commander."

The two men go through the morning protocol, dealing with any matters that need their immediate attention. Finney hands the boss his morning mail then alerts him about the emails that need his attention.

"Say, boss," he adds, "did, you hear anything more about the problems that are stirring up in South America? Is there any chance we might deploy?"

"Nothing but rumors, Finney. Nothing but rumors. Once the politicians decide which side they want to be on, then and only then will we have any chance of settling the problem," David tells him.

About this time, Finney has poured each of them a morning cup of java. When the two have pretty much settled into the day's business routine, he says, "Boss, last night a buddy and I were having a few beers when he asked me a question I had a hard time dealing with. Explaining things to a fellow military person is a whole lot easier than trying to explain the same thing to a civilian."

"What are you getting at, Finney?" asks David.

"Well, you see, this guy knows I am a Navy SEAL, and in his mind he thinks of us as paid military killers. So he asks me, how do I feel about being a paid killer? Honestly, boss, I never really gave it much thought, so when he asked me, it caught me off guard. You know, I really had a hard time with it. How would you have answered the question?"

"Well, Finney, I think it is quite simple. When some big bully is beating up my family or my friends, I have no problem telling the bully to pick on someone their own size. When they refuse, then it is my duty to intervene and put the bully in his proper place. Some bullies simply will not listen to reason, and when that happens, then it just might be necessary to put the bully someplace special. If that is not possible, then I have no problem ending his problem permanently.

"What most civilians don't realize is how much effort goes into trying to find common acceptable ground, before we are called in. In other words, I look at it as a mission, and the needs of the mission are paramount, or our boss would not send us in to finalize the deal to begin with. Finney, I don't ever remember being sent in to specifically kill someone. The killing usually takes place when the bad guys refuse to listen to reason and destroy all other options at our disposal. That again is the part the civilians don't understand—a tremendous effort has taken place before we are asked to settle the situation. I suppose you could use the term 'trained killers' as, technically, that is what we are. And we are the best in the world at doing our job. The more the opposition knows this, the easier our job will be. If they know we are being sent to end a situation, generally they will capitulate before we have to resort to extreme measures since we are, for the most part, covert once the signal is given. Then it's all over but the shouting.

"So you see, this term 'killer' can actually save lives in the long run. To answer your question, yes, I am a killer and a very good one at that. But that is not how I would broadcast about us on national TV. To your buddy, though, yes.

"Finney, tell the team we will have a demo training exercise first thing in the morning at the north beach. This will also be an air insertion, water deployed."

"Sure thing, boss. I'll post the agenda right away," says Finney.

As the day moves on, 1400 hours (or 2:00 PM) comes up pretty fast, and David knows he has to leave for his appointment.

"I have to leave for an appointment at 1400, Finney, so I will see you in the morning," David yells

Out the door he goes and off to his meeting with the doctor. David has made sure no one at the base knows he is going to see a shrink. If word of this got out, it could have an effect on his career. Under no circumstances does David want anyone thinking he might be having mental problems. Visiting a psychiatrist would be difficult to explain. As a leader of a SEAL team, there is no room for maneuvering on this matter, so David takes no chances and keeps it on the QT.

When he arrives in downtown San Diego, it doesn't take long for him to make his way to the medical tower's fifth floor and stand in front of an office door that could put to rest twenty-five years of nightmares. At least he hopes it will. On the other hand, the meeting could very well open another can of worms that David may not be prepared to deal with. Twenty-five years of grief are facing him, so to say that David Adelman is nervous would be an understatement.

Obviously he would like to solve the complete problem, but that is part of the problem: David has no idea what it is that is causing the nightmares. What if the truth turns out to be something that will be detrimental to him and his career?

What if I have done something in the past that could have me committed to jail or prison? he wonders. *Worse yet, since my nightmares come with a lot of screaming, could I be guilty of something really bad? Is it possible I killed someone in my past?* His mind is going ninety MPH from one thing to another; this is not a good time for David. He begins to sweat, his hands are shaking, and he also starts to have second thoughts.

"I am doing the right thing?" he asks himself. "Is this going to ruin my career? Am I liable to have to go to jail? Oh hell. As they say, no guts no glory," he thinks aloud.

He begins to reach for the door knob then quickly withdraws before remembering the promise he made to his wife. Still, he finds that simply opening a door has become one of the hardest things he has had to do in his life. After pulling back from the door several times, he finally reaches for the knob and turns it. As the door opens, David's heart stops beating... Or at least he thinks it did. This 198-pounds of muscle has suddenly turned to 198 pounds of jelly.

David steps through the doorway, his feet like concrete blocks, but soon he sees wall after wall covered with certificates of some kind. He thinks to himself, *If documents of approval and completion of training certificates mean anything then this doctor must be really smart.*

He walks over to the reception desk and says to the receptionist, "I am Commander Adelman, and I am here for my 2:00 appointment."

"Good afternoon, Commander. We have been expecting you. You are right on time. Did you have any trouble finding us?" asks the receptionist

"Not really."

"Please have a seat. The doctor will see you in just a moment."

David continues to really wrestle with this visit. *Well, I have made it this far,* he thinks as he sits on the sofa, *and the world has not come to an end. It is not too late, though. I can always say I have to go. My pager is calling me at the base. What the hell—I am committed. I may as well suck it up and keep my word to my wife.*

In just a few moments a door opens and out walks a very distinguished looking man about fifty-five to sixty years of age. He walks over to David and says, "You must be Commander Adelman."

David stands and puts out his hand to greet the doctor. The two men shake hands and a few pleasantries are exchanged. "Commander, do you mind if I call you David?"

"No, not at all," says David.

"Great. Why don't we go into my office and see if we can make heads or tails out of the problem your wife was trying to explain to me last week. David, would you like a cup of coffee or something cold to drink?"

"Coffee would be fine. Cream only, if you please."

The doctor says, "Well, that is getting off on the right foot—that is how I drink my coffee, also."

David looks around. "Where is the couch?"

"You know, a lot of people ask that very question. I don't have a couch, David. I want the full attention of my clients. I feel that if people want to relax, the hotel down the road is a lot cheaper than I am. Tell me, David, how do you feel about being here in the first place? Just so you know, this visit is confidential between you and me. The military will never know it took place. Again, how do you feel?"

"Honestly, scared. Scared as hell," says David.

"Why?"

"I really wish I knew. All I know is I have bad dreams and have no idea why. I have been having the same dream, over and over, for as long as I can remember."

"How long, have you been having this dream?"

"Not sure. As best I can put a time frame on it, I would say it goes back to my childhood. Exactly when they started, though, can't say."

"Okay, tell me as much about the dream as you can. Try not to leave anything out," says the doctor.

"There is not much to it. I hear what appear to be screams. I am not sure, but if I were to take a guess, I would say they were female screams. Again, not sure, but I think there is more than one person. This breaks me out into a very heavy sweat, and then I find myself reaching out to them and yelling, '*Stop!*' It is at this time that I always wake up. Doc, this scares the hell out of me, as I have no idea what it is about. I keep thinking I may be responsible for something really bad."

"You're not the first person to have that feeling after coming through that door. It is natural to fear the unknown. Tell me, just how far back in your life can you remember?"

"Not too sure about that, either," says David.

"David, I notice, on your arm, you have a number tattooed there. This is similar to the numbering system found on Holocaust victims from

World War Two. Is there any connection?" asks the doctor.

"Yes, I do remember having this number, and I can pinpoint it to the war era. I do remember being at a prison camp called Dachau, and I also remember being stripped of my clothes and standing in line to take a shower. That's what the guards said was about to take place. In hindsight, I am sure I was in line to be gassed, along with about 150 other children. Just about the time that we were ready to be led into the shower, gunfire erupted outside the compound and the U.S. Army showed up. I now realize that that is what saved my life. This occurred April twenty-fourth, 1945, about mid-afternoon. I later checked, and it turns out the 42nd and the 45th Army Divisions were the units involved in our liberation."

"Can you remember back any further than that date?"

"No, not a single moment."

The doctor asks, "How about after the liberation?"

"Yes, I can pretty much lay out my history from there on. I was taken by the MYPP."

"What was that?"

"The Military Youth Placement Program, and after about six months, I was shipped to the U.S., where they did all kinds of processing of us kids. I got shots and medical checkups, and then I was placed in a foster home 'til I turned eighteen. Turns out I was one of the lucky ones. You see, my foster parents actually loved me and treated me as one of their original family. A lot of the kids placed in foster homes bounced from home to home.

"I later went to college, thanks to my new adopted family, where I also attended an ROTC program. After about five years of college, I graduated with a degree in business then joined the U.S. Navy as a Naval Officer. That is where I have been for the last eleven or so years."

"That, David, is a good overview of your life, and I think it is going to work in our favor. You see, we are mainly dealing with a time bracket that starts with you being about nine years old, so I think we can pretty much rule out your being a mass murderer. David, I think it is going to come down to some event or thing that happened in your life that you are trying to block out. What that is, I am not sure we will ever know exactly, but I think we should be able to put your fear of life itself to bed.

"When your wife called and gave me an overview of your problem, I had my staff do some homework. They spent time checking your background and past history as best we could. We are very sure you are, as

I said earlier, not a mass murder, and I really don't think you have any dark corners in your life, at least not after the war. I feel certain that what we are looking for lies during the years of age nine and under. It could even be more specific and have occurred very close in time to the moment just prior to the Germans' attempt to execute you. Do you have any memory at all of your parents?"

"No, none."

"Well, one thing is for sure."

"What's that?" asks David

"You did have parents. Now all we have to do is track them down and see if they are part of the puzzle. We know you were raised somewhere in Europe, so that is our starting point. If we get lucky, the military might have recovered some German documents that can help us. As bad as the Germans were, they did have a desire to keep records. I cannot promise you we will find what we are looking for, but I will promise you we will try."

The doctor continues, "David, my history with these types of cases, where someone is afraid they are a killer, a thief, or just generally a bad guy, is that, once you put the ultimate problem to rest, my patients seem to be able to live a more normal life. It's too early to say how far we will be able to take your problem, but my guess is you will start to sleep a little more soundly. The fact that you remember your original name is going to be a big help. I will be in contact with you within a few weeks."

"Thanks, Doc. I really do feel better already. I'll look forward to hearing from you," David says as he walks out the door.

As he leaves, he turns back to look at the door knob, touches it, and says to it, "You're not as big and bad as I made you out to be."

He heads for home, and as he walks through the door, he greets his kids and wife, Loraine. She looks at him and says, "All right, lay it on me. What did the doc say, and how do you feel about the meeting?"

David steps back and takes a deep breath then says, "You know, I really do feel good about the meeting, and this guy is sharp. He said some neat things and kind of put my mind at ease, at least for now. The proof of the pudding is going to be in the tasting. I guess we will just have to wait and see how it all plays out. Given how often I have this stupid dream, I don't think we will have to wait long to find out."

CHAPTER 2

The mid 1930s found the continent of Europe beginning to make significant changes. The country of Germany was the reason behind many of them. The whole world was anxiously watching them to see what was going to happen. The Nazi party had become more and more powerful, causing a lot of people to rethink their politics as well as how they were going to live their lives.

The Jewish community of Germany and Poland was probably the most concerned, as they were the largest group being persecuted. During this time period, thousands of Jews left Germany, trying to find safer territory. Like most intelligent parents and business owners, the Jewish community was busy making arrangements for their families as best they could.

One didn't have to be a genius to realize that something bad was coming down. One family in particular was the Adelman family.

Two brothers, Abe Adelman of Hamburg and his older brother Ben Adelman of Berlin, both started to make arrangements for their two families to be able to survive if things should become unmanageable, which was beginning to look like it might become a reality.

It was becoming obvious to a lot of people that the country, for them, was not taking a very good direction. Few had the slightest idea of what was in store for them.

Ben was the more successful of the two brothers and by the mid-1930s had amassed quite a fortune in the precious metals industry. He had been making financial investments in different businesses right along for quite a while. Fearing that something might happen that could cost him, his life's work, and his fortune, Ben decided to travel to Switzerland and make arrangements to protect his assets. He planned to just possibly establish a protocol that he would be able to fall back on, should his family develop the need to leave the country.

Ben traveled to Switzerland and, after careful consideration, chose the Zurich National Bank to do his business with.

Ben told the bank president, "I'm not sure how things in Germany are going to turn out, so I would like to prepare for the worst."

The bank president introduced Ben to a Mr. Sven Haldiman, who would be Ben's account manager. Mr. Haldiman started to draw up Mr. Adelman's account instructions, telling him, "This is where your money will be and how it will be protected."

He also gave him the necessary procedures for making withdrawals, be they local or by wire.

Ben read it all over with extreme anxiety, but for some reason he began to get a feeling of comfort as he studied the paperwork carefully. The document read almost, Ben realized, as if he might never see the account again. The two worked over the document several times before Ben was comfortable with it.

Ben asked Mr. Haldiman, "Is the account time-sensitive, for security purposes?"

"Mr. Adelman, I can assure you, this account will be intact for the next several hundred years, if you so wish it," the account manager stated.

"Fine. It looks like a good plan."

The two also discussed an agreement whereby the bank's investment team would look after Ben's accounts and make what they believed to be sound financial investments, in an attempt to grow the account. The account agent gave Ben a full description of how and where the investment team worked and what their past history had been. Ben was very satisfied with this information and excited to know that someone was looking after his family's interests.

Ben asked, "Since I am not sure how it is that I will want to execute withdrawals from the account, or even when I may do it, I would like to set up a few key passwords and signatures as protection for the account."

Mr. Haldiman assured Ben, "That is not a problem."

At that point the two of them agreed on an account number, and Ben signed signature release cards for examination for when any situation required such verification.

Having completed his duty in Zurich, Ben headed for home, hoping things would work out the way he wanted them to and sincerely hoping that his fears were just that: fears. Unfortunately, the Nazi party continued to make miserable for almost all Jews in Berlin, as they were throughout the rest of the country. It was apparent that the country was going downhill rather quickly.

Upon arriving home, Ben contacted his brother and suggested he bring his entire family to Berlin where, hopefully, he could bring his influence and wealth to bear on protecting the family.

Abe saw the message and agreed with his brother. Hamburg was swiftly becoming a hunting ground for Jews, so he saw many advantages to leaving and joining his brother.

The entire Adelman family—Abe, his wife, his young son David and his two teenage daughters—packed up and headed for Berlin. What they saw happening on the streets as they travelled to Berlin was frightening. The children cried practically throughout the entire trip. Time was slipping by, and the country for the Jewish populace was growing worse. No one seemed to be safe anymore, and everyone was scrambling for any kind of security they could find, which by that point was not much.

Ben was paying off the local politicians, and as a result had achieved some resemblance of security for himself and his brother's family. But Ben was beginning to wonder how much longer he would be able to protect them all. Just how long could they stay out of sight of the Nazis and the SS? Every day more and more Jews were being rounded up and taken away. No one seemed to know where they were being taken, so a state of panic was fast setting in.

###

The year was 1943, and the country had been at war for several years. Most of the Jews had been taken away, to where no one seemed to know. What was happening to them, again, no one was sure but rumors abounded.

It was costing Ben more and more money each month to protect his family, but he was eagerly willing to pay it if it bought them the protection they seemed to be getting from it.

However, one day, he had to sit down at the table with his brother Abe and tell him, "I don't think we are going to be able to hold out much longer. I suggest you meet with your family and try to put some kind of plan together for how you all will handle the situation when the time comes and they take us all away."

Abe was quite shaken by this news, but it was not something he was unaware might come about. The family sat down and discussed what they hoped was a plan, knowing full well that they would not have any say in what happened to them when and if the Nazis came and take them away.

Abe explained to his family, "No matter what happens, life is paramount. No matter what happens to us or what they make us do, time will heal everything. But if we are dead, then nothing can happen and there is nothing to rebuild on."

Abe felt certain they would be split up, so he continued, "If at all possible, you two girls try to stay with your mother. And my precious David, you stay with your mother, also. I will need you to protect her. Can you do that?"

Young David looked at his father, not completely understanding what was taking place, but he did know that things were not good and assured his father that, at eight years of age, he was man enough to protect them.

Abe looked at David with a smile that stretched from ear to ear, feeling an extreme amount of pride. He said, "I know you are. That is why I have given you this important job."

All one had to do was look out the window to see that times were getting tougher and meaner in Berlin. Within two weeks of that family meeting, the Adelmans were home having dinner together when the door was knocked completely off its hinges. In barged six German SS soldiers. They grabbed the entire family and dragged them out of the building and down the street to two awaiting large trucks. The family members were pushed into the trucks, and a trip to the train yard began. Obviously they were all crying and yelling but to no avail.

Upon reaching the train station, the entire truckload of people were herded into box cars until each car was so full, you could not put one more person inside of it. This was then followed by an eight-hour train ride.

The conditions in the box cars were deplorable. Prisoners could not even go to a bathroom to relieve themselves. Instead, they simply did it while standing where they were; there was absolutely no other choice. It didn't take long before the stench in the box cars became unbearable.

Berlin is in the northeastern part of Germany while Dachau Prison was southeast, down at the other end of the country. A couple of elders died en route to the prison camp, but no one knew they were dead until they arrived at the prison and began unloading the box cars. They simply died standing on their feet; that's where they were until the end of the trip.

This was the beginning of what would be a short, frightening period of pain and anguish for the Adelman family. Just as they suspected, as soon as the train arrived, the families were split up. The men went one way, and the women and children another. As they separated, this was the last time the men ever saw their loved ones again. They were herded into very small, tight quarters in buildings that were like barracks, long and not very wide.

Dachau prison was a place where prisoners became forced labor for the munitions factory that was on site. As long as you were able to do work, you were allowed to live.

If you became sick or disabled, however, you were shot or worse, as the German guards saw fit.

Ben and Abe were fortunate in that they both were put in the same barracks. They, at least, had some companionship of family. They would be able to enjoy this situation just so long as the Germans did not find out. Since they never knew who was a turncoat and might tell on them, they made sure that no one knew about their relationship. They were simply two men who knew each other, and even with the closeness they shared with each other, fortunately no one ever figured out their relationship.

Dachau was designed as a base for a work force to work in the munitions factory, but at the same time it was used as a training site for future SS prison guards.

This training facility was what really turned out to be bad. The guards learn their cruelty trade there and then exported it elsewhere. As could be expected, people started dying right away. The extreme elderly didn't have a chance. Only the reasonably strong would survive, and as time went on, even their chances of survival became less and less.

Malnutrition and disease ran rampant in the camp and claimed many new lives every day. One would think that sooner or later there wouldn't be any more workers, but the trains kept coming, and each train brought a fresh crop of workers and death.

The prisoners found the living conditions deplorable, but at the same time, if that was all they had to contend with, they felt they might still have a chance. But when you factored in the brutality of the prison's SS guards, then you knew your time was limited. The guards were not only cruel and ruthless, but they did their torture and punishments with such a pleasure. To kill someone with a club or a bayonet was one thing, but they made a game out of it by laughing out loud and claiming, "I can kill my man, faster than you can kill yours."

By this time, Abe and Ben had come to the realization that they were not going to get out of

Dachau alive. Survival was not in the cards for them, and there was nothing they could do about it.

One day, Abe said to Ben, "You know we are not going to survive this ordeal."

"Yes, I am well aware of it, my brother," said Ben.

Abe looked at his brother and said, "Ben, I have an idea. We may not be able to do anything about these bastards now, but I have an idea for how, with a little luck, we just might be able to get even with them later in life"

"Go ahead. I am all ears. What is your plan?"

Abe said, "I have been keeping track of the guards who I think are the really cruel ones and the ones who deserve retribution. I believe there are about fifteen of them. I am not saying that others don't deserve punishment as well, but these fifteen are the worst of the worst. Ben, I suggest we write their names down in a book or a diary-like book, and list everything we can find out about them. Then we can hide the book in hopes that, someday, if we are lucky, someone just might find the book and listed atrocities, and then be able to track them down and execute revenge on them on our behalf. I know it is a long shot, but quite frankly what else can we do?"

Now that the idea of revenge had been born, new life seemed to have been injected into Abe and Ben and the few others they recruited to help them execute their plan.

With the plan in place, the five or six guys that Abe and Ben had befriended set about working it.

The idea was to strike up as many conversations as they could, from time to time, with the guards or others who know the guards. Their objective was to find out first their names, then where they were from, their home towns, any family members, and as much other information as they could extract.

This list of information then went into the book that Abe was in charge of creating. It was he who did the entry writing.

The men searched wide and far in the barracks to find a place to hide the book when it was not being used for writing entries. Finally, one day, someone called their attention to the end of one of the bunk beds. It seemed that the ends of the boards were joined through the mortise and tenon-type of joint construction, and that part of the tenon on one end board had been broken off, leaving a gap or space in the end of the other board that was the mortise.

This gap was just big enough to conceal the small diary when placed inside it. They could pull the board out, put the book in, and then slide the broken board back in place. No one could tell the difference.

There was no lack of desire for names to place on the retribution list. One name at the top of everyone's mind was a guard known as the butcher.

The butcher was about six feet tall and overweight. This SS guard had a really bad sense of humor. His idea of fun was to take his bayonet and inflict a cut or gash in some prisoner and then, over time, watch gangrene set in and eventually kill the man with severe pain. So "Conrad Kaiser," as the butcher was named, became the number-one candidate on their hit list. As it turned out, he was also the head guard of their camp.

There were several others who came close to the top spot, but the group was in agreement that he belonged in the number-one position. As an SS guard, one had to wonder what it must have been like to have so many people go to bed each night praying for your death. It didn't take long for the list to grow; it finally became their list of fifteen. Each time Abe placed a new candidate on the list, he include as much information as he could acquire in order to support the prisoners' claims.

Abe and Ben both were surprised to discover how much information could be gotten on these men and the relative ease with which it came to them. They soon found out, when talking to the guards, that they too were homesick and, given the opportunity to talk about home, were just as eager as anyone else to divulge information in the form of small talk.

Little did these men realize that they were signing their death warrants with this small talk about home. Soon, beside every name was a list of the atrocities each had committed, and in some cases, Abe would give them a personal name of his choosing to match the person's character, such as the "butcher" and the "maniac." Then there was a camp favorite: "Mr. Stupid Shit." The list of names was quite ingenious. There was "big lips" and "pug nose," and, of course, another camp favorite, "Asshole."

Ben got seriously involved with the book as did Abe, and during one of the entry sessions, Ben noticed that on the back of the book, the cover was coming loose. Upon close examination, Ben realized this would make a great place for him to hide some of his personal information. Since this whole scheme hinged upon the luck of someone someday in the future finding it and reacting to the information, he got to thinking that he just might have an avenue by which he, with luck, might be able to pass on his vast financial fortune in the hopes that someday it could be used for good in the world.

CHAPTER 3

Life was miserable for all. The men were, in their small and unique way, trying to fight back. What was going on with the women was just shared in whispers here and there; but no one was really sure what was fact and what was fiction. The atrocities around them were blood-curdling, but there was nothing they could do. Hope and prayer were their biggest weapons.

One day, Ben was talking to someone who lived in one of the barracks that was reasonably close to the women's barracks.

The man knew the Adelman family and, when he had the chance, told Ben, "I have some really bad news about Abe's family. You know, the guards routinely take the female prisoners to a special building and then rape them... This is pretty routine. Of course, the beautiful ones are in great demand, but they can only take so much. Last week, the guards found out that this one woman had two teenage daughters and they were both good looking.

They thought this would be a great opportunity to have fun with the whole family, so they took Abe's wife and two teenage daughters to this building and severely raped all three of them. When done, they decided it would be fun to have the kids watch their mother die in front of them. After they did so, they killed the two girls, as well."

Abe continued, "It was also found out that Abe's wife took her nine-year-old son David with her everywhere she went. Well, Ben, I am afraid that David was witness to the whole ordeal. Why they let him live, I don't know, but they did."

Ben went back to his barracks, the burden almost too much for him. *How was he going to handle this?* he wondered to himself.

For the longest time after that, he was not the same, and Abe soon began to notice this difference, so he asked his brother, "What is the matter, Ben? I know times are tough, but you are not yourself lately."

Ben snapped back at him, "Leave me alone. I don't want to talk about it."

This really caught Abe by surprise. This did not seem like his brother talking. Something must have happened recently that had a great effect on Ben, but Ben refused to discuss anything about the painful discoveries with Abe. Abe did continue to pester his brother to try and find out what was bothering him.

At this point, Ben had decided that telling his brother about the rape and death of his wife and two daughters was not going to accomplish anything. All it would do was give poor Abe more depression than he already had to deal with. Ben decided to take this knowledge with him to the grave. The only salvation or ray of hope for the two brothers had was in continuing their diary and inputting as much information as possible in hopes that, someday, someone else might dispense the retribution needed.

Ben got to thinking about the hidden back cover of the diary and how he might be able to make use of it. The whole idea of the diary was based upon luck, so why not reach out for a little more? Ben decided to write out his last will and testament, along with a few other notes, and put them in the back of the diary before restitching the binding so that no one would know they were there.

Ben started on his will.

This is Ben Adelman of Berlin, former owner of the Adelman Jewelry Company. This is to be my last will and testament and supersedes any prior claims to my estate, dated 1944, January 22.

Attached are several signatures of prison friends of mine who are acting as witnesses to this document.

Realizing that I will not survive this ordeal here at Dachau prison, and that I do not honestly believe any of my family will, either, with this in mind I am attaching the necessary information for the finder of this document to go to Switzerland and, at the Zurich National Bank, present this to the account manager of my account.

My account number is 75977XK72311M2. This number, along with the copy of my signature below, should give you complete ownership of my estate.

Since you can only have this will through the fact that you are also in possession of this diary that has been kept by my brother, Abe Adelman, it is assumed you have read the diary thoroughly and have been made witness to the atrocities committed upon our entire family.

My wish is that you or someone whom you may desire to hire will take the list contained within of these vicious German criminals and exact as much retribution upon them as is humanly possible.

I ask this not only for my own family, but for the thousands upon thousands of others who were severely mistreated and tortured by these brutal men.

I realize I can't enforce my desires upon you, but I appeal to your sense of humanity, justice, and fairness.

Attached are the names of men who have been prisoners with us and who have endured these atrocities along with us. If, by chance, one or more of these men's immediate family members survive the war, then I would ask you to consider sharing a portion of your financial gain with them, so that it might give them a chance at starting a new life.

Sincerely,

Ben Adelman

###

Then he included this list of The Friends of Ben and Abe Adelman:

Jacob Feinstein
Alexander Maier
Arthur Schaber
Solomon Berkowitz
Alfred Schatzman

Finally, he wrote this:

This note is attached to this document as a follow up, as it is of a very personal nature.

These SS men during one incident in particular raped and killed my brother Abe Adelman's wife and two teenage daughters and, during the incident, required his nine-year-son David to witness the entire event.

If there is any justice in this history of events, then so may there be retribution for these men.

Ben was right: none of the family lived to the end of the war, so none knew how their wishes would play out.

CHAPTER 4

The war has been over now for about twenty-four years, and there has been a lot of activity around what soon became known as the Holocaust. Even this many years after the fact, however, the Holocaust is still talked about in whispers. To this very day there are those who refuse to believe it actually happened.

Some wanted to tear down Dachau Prison and burn everything, while others believed that preserving part of it as a museum is a better idea, so that it would act as a reminder to future generations of what has happened in the past. The European Historical Society became involved and decided to keep part of the Dachau Prison as a museum for future awareness. Their plan involved trying to save as much of the remaining facility as possible.

One day, the work crews were working diligently on the inside of the barracks one day. They decided to carry the bunk beds outside in order to better evaluate the condition of everything. As they were carrying this one particular bunk structure, they happened to bump it into another stack of beds already outside. With the impact of the two bunks colliding, one of them came apart.

The boss yelled at the worker, "We are here to preserve this stuff, not destroy it."

"Yeah, yeah, I hear ya'," said the worker. But as he went over to stick the board back into its original slot, he noticed something inside the hole where the board was supposed to go. He reached in and pulled out this little book. What he didn't know at that moment was that he had just recovered Abe Adelman's diary.

The worker gave his boss a call, "Come look at what I just found."

The boss walked over to the bed and looked at the book but didn't really pay it much attention.

"Tell you what you do with that. Tag it, just like all the rest of the gear and equipment we have been finding, and let the Historical people decide what to do with it."

The diary was then put in a box, along with several hundred other very small artifacts, and delivered to the main office of the Historical Society. Given the extreme number of items that were found, the process of identification and design had gotten pretty boring. Quite a few items were mishandled, put into storage boxes, and marked for future investigation. The box with the diary was tagged and labeled, as were the items in it. It was then put on a storage shelf for someone else to look at someday in the future, if and when the Society received enough money to follow up on its work.

About a year went by and the Historical Society finished with its charter to preserve the Dachau Prison. It opened as a museum and received a tremendous number of tourist visits each month. As time passes, one can only imagine how the ghosts of the museum must be turning in their graves, waiting for that diary to surface and for the inevitable retribution to be enacted upon those who so deserve it.

As promised, Dr. Flarity sends a team of research specialists out into the field to try and find out as much as they can about David and his family, if any members are still alive. He is determined to find out why David is having these severe nightmares, and specifically why it is the same dream over and over.

Karen Black is the assistant researcher whom the doctor has assigned to this case, and she is a very accomplished researcher at that.

Karen goes to Germany and the Dachau Prison in the hopes of finding something—anything. She realizes that she doesn't have a lot to go on, but since David has no known relatives, where else can she start? She knows that this is the site of David's last memories, and seemingly of his only ones.

When asked about his life, David said that he only remembers being naked, in line to take a shower, which we now know was supposed to be the gas chamber, but that the American soldiers arrived just in time to prevent the murder of some 150 young children.

Karen begins by asking everyone at the museum whether there are any records of the prison back when it was active.

The custodians tell her, "There are all kinds of records. Most are posted on the walls around the museum for the public to see and read."

After several hours of wandering through the museum and reading all the messages and memos that are posted, she is certain that there is nothing there of interest for her and her project.

She then goes back to the entrance desk and asks, "Are there any other documents or memorabilia?"

The person sitting at the desk says, "I don't know of anything extra."

It is about this time that an elderly man, a security guard standing nearby, speaks up and says, "You might want to go to the Historical Society and see if they have anything else that has not been put on display. They were the ones who uncovered all this that you see on display here."

Karen thanks the gentleman and then heads for the Historical Society in hopes of finding something.

Upon entering the Historical Society building, Karen finds the person who is in charge of the fact-finding project for discovering information about the Dachau Prison. She asks, "Might I have a few minutes of tour time? Maybe buy you a coffee?"

Another young lady extends her hand to greet Karen. "I was the person in charge of the research for the renovation of the prison and making of it into a museum for future generations to see. Have you been to the museum yet?"

Karen answers, "Yes, but unfortunately I didn't find anything that shed light on the research project that I am involved in." She wonders, "Is there anything left that is not on display that came from the prison?"

"No, I believe we have put out everything that we uncovered. I am pretty sure of it, but I tell you what. Give me a few moments, and I will go upstairs and look in the research room where we keep the items from Dachau. Let me see if there is anything left over."

Karen says, "Thank you so much, I really appreciate you taking your time on this."

After about ten minutes, the lady comes back downstairs carrying a very small box. She sets it on the table, and the two ladies begin to search through the hodgepodge of nick knacks inside. In the process, Karen reaches down, pulls out a very small booklet out, and opens it. As she begins to read the book, it isn't but a matter of minutes before she realizes that this is the diary of her client's father. Karen realizes she has found exactly what she was looking for. Her face lights up as if she had just found a pot of solid gold. But now she has another problem.

These are historical documents, so surely the Society was not going to let her walk out the door with them. Karen tries to explain to the lady in charge the importance of the little book, but as she suspected, they are not allowed to let anything leave the archive. In fact, there is protocol in place for just such a case so, if Karen were to contact her superior, she would learn how to start the claiming process.

Later that day, when it was morning time back in the States, Karen calls her boss Dr. Flarity and breaks the good news. "I think I have found what you are looking for. It appears to be a personal diary, and it is written by our client's father. All I have to do is finish the paperwork that will allow us to take possession of it and then it will be ours."

"Great. How soon do you think you will have the document?" asks the doctor.

"I have the necessary paperwork, but I have to go to the U.S. Embassy and get a document stamped with the proper release. Then it's back to the Historical Society to pick up the book and then catch the big bird back home. I hope to be in your office tomorrow afternoon."

"Great! Good work, Karen. This calls for a little bonus."

Dr. Flarity calls David to give him the good news. He tells him, "The book, or diary, is still in Europe, but my assistant will have it back here in the States in a couple of days."

The doctor is not completely honest about the exact arrival date of the book will. He wants to have at least one day to study the item in order to see if there is enough information in it to put David's dreams to rest.

David puts down the phone and tells his wife, "Good news."

Loraine is jumping with joy, as is David. At this point in his life, this diary is going to be the only thing he has that belonged to his father. To be able to read his father's comments at such a perilous time in all their lives will be tremendous.

He tells his wife, "It is going to be a long two days."

The flight feels long, as Karen is anxious to show what she has found. During the flight, she studies the book and is impressed with the information in it, At the same time, though, she's aghast at the inhumanity that the prisoners had to endure. She wonders to herself how could one human being be so cruel and do so much to others?

As soon as she arrives back, she and the doctor begin to go over the diary's contents.

Dr. Flarity looks at Karen and says, "This is a really great find for David, but I am not so sure there is anything in it that is going to solve his problem."

"That is the same conclusion I came to on the airplane," Karen says. "There is a lot in it, and it's surely a great piece of history, but what does it do for David?"

"It is going to be interesting how he responds to this. Myself, I am hoping that just having something in his hands that belonged to his father will be enough to with draw him away from the terrible dreams," the doctor comments. "But we won't know until we try it."

CHAPTER 5

David and his wife arrive at the doctor's office. The receptionist receives them and tells them, "The doctor will see you in just a moment."

"Welcome, Mrs. Adelman," Dr. Flarity says as she ushers them in. "And how are you today, David?"

They all shake hands, and the doctor hands them each a cup of coffee. "I assume you are anxious to see your father's diary."

"That's an understatement," says David.

"Well, here it is." He hands David the small book.

David just stands there in awe for the longest time. "Do you realize this is the only thing I have that used to belong to my father? I don't even have a picture of the man. I have no idea what he looked like. Was he a big man? A little man? What do you suppose his personality was like? This is information that most men and women take for granted as just part of their everyday life. Yet I have none of it. Just this little book, written during a time of extreme stress in his life."

The doctor looks at him. "David, I have read the diary. It is powerful and demanding, but I am not sure there is anything in it that will end your dreams. I guess that only time will tell. I am hoping that the presence of your father's spirit will reach out and touch you enough to help you with your problem."

"Well, Doc, we are going to find out pretty soon. I really want to thank you for your efforts. I think you have gone the extra mile in dealing with my situation. Let's hope it works out."

David and his wife Loraine thank the doctor again and leave.

When David gets home, he sits down at the kitchen table and just stares at the diary. It takes them almost fifteen minutes to work up the courage to open it, his anticipation is so great. He tells his wife, "I am afraid to open it. Will it tell me what my father was? Or what the Nazis turned him into?"

Again, David continues to just stare. Finally he opens the book and starts to read the diary. It isn't long, and he realizes he is looking at his father's wish list. It is not a description of the daily routines that he thought it was going to be. David was hoping that the book would describe something he could relate to, that the entries would paint a picture of his father and give him something to bond with.

After carefully studying the diary and getting a thorough understanding of what was in front of him, David tells his wife, "This is a list of atrocities committed by a list of very bad people, and my father's desire to get even with them."

David stares at the text some more. In it, his father has reached out from the grave and asked him, as his son, to help him. But there is absolutely nothing David can do.

He holds the book in his hands for the longest time and then starts to cry. The only time his father has ever asked him for help and David cannot do it. Loraine tries to comfort him, but it doesn't seem to do much good, as he continues to bawl like a baby. Getting the diary was certainly a high point for David, but realizing what it is asking of him takes the wind out of him.

###

After a few days of dealing with the issue, David and Loraine are discussing the diary when she looks at her husband and says, "David, there is no way this book was meant to be in your hands. At the time this was written, you were only nine years old. Your father was hoping someone—anyone—would get the book and dish out the necessary punishment deserved by these men. There is absolutely no way for him to have known that it would fall into *your* hands, let alone at an age when you could have done something."

David looks at her. "I suppose you're right, honey. I fully agree with everything you said, but just the same, it did wind up with me. So now, what do I do about it?"

After several days of reading and rereading the diary and trying to get used to his father's spiritual presence, David finally begins to settle down. His emotions no longer take him on a roller coaster ride, and he becomes sure that, in due time, he will decide upon the proper course he needs to travel. At the moment, however, it is time to get back into the groove of the business at hand, and that means dealing with bad guys of the present day.

David shows up at the office and has started to get acclimated to the normal routine again when his buddy Finney shows up. "Hey, Finney, you know how you ask me how it feels to be a killer?"

"Yeah. So what's up? Got someone you want me to kill?" says Finney

"No, you smart ass. I've got an interesting story to share with you," says David.

With this, he starts to tell Finney about getting his father's twenty-five-year old diary and what it contained. The one thing he is sure not to reveal, though, is his history of bad dreams and the recent doctor visits.

"Don't you think it odd that what my father wants done is exactly what we do for a living, yet this is one case we can't touch?" asks David.

Finney pauses for a moment, "Yeah, it does kind of have an ironic swing to it. Now that you mention it, how are you handling this, talking to your father from the grave? Seems awful spooky to me."

"You know, Finney, even if someone could respond to the ideas that my father expresses in the diary, how could you do it? It would cost a fortune to track all those men down and to find out not only where they are, but who is still alive and who isn't. Then comes the big question—how would you go about treating the issue? Do you track them down and then turn them over to the law, so they can pick them up and then levy war crimes judgments on them? Or do you kill them as you locate them? By the time you were done killing all those men, you would be known as the Dachau mass murder. Man, what a large sum of money it would take."

###

Life for David Adelman starts to get back on track and some sense of normality begins to grab hold of him again. He is back to Navy business and taking the kids to karate lessons and Little League, even if it is just still T-ball. Life around the house is back to normal and goes on pretty much as expected for a couple of months, with nothing out of the ordinary.

Then one night he is again asleep and everything looks normal, but then the nightmare arrives once more. It isn't long before David is covered in sweat again, fighting off the terrible deeds that are taking place in his mind. After the familiar tossing and turning, he finally sits up in bed, reaches out, and yells, "Stop! *Stop! Please stop!*"

Loraine grabs him and hugs him very tightly. That is when they both realize that this matter has not be put to rest.

The next morning, as they sit having their morning coffee together, they both look at each other and can see despair in each other's eyes.

"I really thought the diary might help. I was so hoping it would," David comments.

"I know, hun. So was I."

He looks at Loraine and says, "There has to be more to this than just what is in the diary and the atrocities that my father experienced. There has to be more."

Loraine looks at her husband and says, "We have come this far fighting this monster, we will travel the miles needed to win this fight. We are not giving up."

After that, life for David and his family continues to return pretty much to normal. It is interesting to note that, although the dreams do not stop, they seem to be a little less frequent. For this, Loraine and David are grateful.

From time to time, David will be setting in his favorite TV chair at home, and he will reach over and pick up the diary just to study it and kind of do some wishful thinking. Sometimes you would think it was a puppy, the way David holds it and strokes it, waiting for something to jump out at him. Almost as if he is waiting for some great revelation to guide him on a trip.

On one particular evening, David is studying the diary again and sees that a string that holds the cover on has started to unravel. It's a little white, rather dirty string that, after all these years, is holding together the cover on the book. He decides to try and fix it but, in his amateurish style, makes the situation worse, and he realizes it.

"Damn it to hell," he says. "All I have done is make it worse. Now I will need to restring the entire binding."

As he starts to pull the string out to facilitate the planned repairs, he notices something odd at the very bottom. He turns the book over and looks very closely at the break in the binding. As he stares at it very hard, he sees, and sure as hell, something is in there.

He yells to Loraine, "Come look at this! There is something in the book cover!"

Loraine searches the stitching with her eyes as well and agrees with David. She says, "Take it out."

"I am going to, honey, but I don't want to destroy the diary itself."

Ever so slowly, David begins to cut a few strands of the binding string. Each cut opens the hole a little wider until they are finally able to pull the extra piece of paper out of the diary.

To say that David and Loraine are engrossed in this would be an understatement. Their eyeballs are about to fall out of their head, staring at the document, as it slides out. When it is finally free of the cover, they ever so carefully start to open the document and begin to read it.

Loraine screams as she hugs her husband. "Do you know what you have here, honey?"

"I think so, yes. But you know, until we contact this bank that is mentioned, we won't know exactly."

"For God sake, keep your fingers crossed," shouts Loraine, because she is certain that they have discovered the last will and testament of David's uncle, Ben Adelman.

After several minutes of digesting the last will and testament, they begin to understand who this man is and why he is doing what he is doing.

"This is my Uncle Ben Adelman, my father's brother, and this list of people names their close friends, men they knew during their ordeal at Dachau."

Their excitement runs wild. Of course, they have yet to find out what the inheritance is or how much.

David looks at Loraine and says, "Honey, please don't get your expectations up too high. Remember, this was a long time ago, and I really don't know how successful Uncle Ben was. We don't even know if this bank is still in existence. Maybe it folded during the war, in which case this is worth nothing."

"I understand," says Loraine. "But it sure is fun to wish."

"If I were to take a guess, I would think, he probably stashed away a few thousand dollars. I would be shocked if it were more than twenty-five to fifty thousand, at the very most. Keep in mind, we would need to honor his request of sharing this with any of his friends' surviving family members. But something is better than nothing."

Loraine says, "I know, honey, but you do have to admit, this is pretty exciting."

David starts the process of trying to find the bank in Switzerland and then the account agent mentioned in the will. The bank in Zurich receives his call and assures him that the person he needs to talk to will contact him within the next twenty -our hours. The bank executive takes David's name and address and the necessary phone number to reestablish contact with him.

David says to Loraine, "Well, at least we know the bank didn't fold during the war. That's a good point in our favor."

About midmorning on the next day, David receives a phone call from the Zurich National Bank and the account agent for David's—or rather, for his uncle's—account.

"Hello, Mr. Adelman?"

"Yes, this is David Adelman."

"Superb. Mr. Adelman I am the account agent for the account in question. I am Christian Krobenberg. The original agent was a Mr. Simon Berlinger, but Mr. Berlinger passed away some years back. Therefore, I will be your contact here at the bank. I will be handling all the transactions necessary to complete anything you desire. Mr. Adelman, the bank will need you to present yourself in person for at least the very first transaction, and that meeting will enable us to make you the controller of the estate. Is this going to be a problem?"

"No, not at all. I will travel to Switzerland within the week, but you see, being in the military, I have to get an authorized leave of absence from my superiors first. If there are any problems with that, I will contact you, and we can make new arrangements," says David.

"Splendid. We will look forward to meeting you here at the bank within the coming week."

David's curiosity is killing him, so he asks Mr. Krobenberg, "Can you tell me what the account is valued at?"

"Well, sir, I don't have the totals here in front of me, but I think it is safe to say it is rather reasonable in size."

"Thank you, Mr. Krobenberg. See you shortly."

Loraine is about to have a litter of kittens, she is so excited—jumping around and yelling, laughing and cheering as she bounces around the room.

"Calm down, woman!" David yells. "We still don't know how much it is worth. A 'reasonable amount' could be anything."

"I know. But you are just as excited as I am, just too prudish to show it, aren't you? Go on. Admit it," Says Loraine.

"Well, maybe."

The next day, David arrives at work at the naval base and immediately goes to see his superior in order to request a short leave.

"Sir, it seems I have inherited an estate of some significance from an uncle who died in the Holocaust. I have to travel to Switzerland to claim it. Might I have a short leave of, say, one week?"

"Not a problem, Commander. I will have my secretary draw it up right now. Sit down and have a cup of coffee while she does the work."

David sits and starts to give his captain a little history of what is going on and how it all came about. Of course, the part about the doctor's visit is not mentioned.

"Well, Commander, did they tell you how much you will be getting? Are you going to remember us poor people when you're rich and famous?"

"Sir, I really don't know what the estate is valued at yet. The bank agent did say it was reasonable in size, whatever the hell that means."

Within a few minutes the secretary has completed David's request for a short leave of absence. She hands it to the captain, and he takes out his pen and applies his required signature. The captain wishes David good luck on his coming trip.

Back home, David and Loraine act like two school kids about to open their Christmas gifts. They have begun to get very giddy, and their imagination is running rampant, but David tries to keep his expectations at around forty to fifty thousand dollars.

Loraine tells David, "For God's sake, don't lose the letter."

As the airplane for Switzerland starts to roll down the runway, David starts to think—or at least hope—that within twelve hours or so, he will be reasonably wealthy. At this point in David's career, it would not take a lot of money to make him feel wealthy, so just about anything is going to be exciting.

All through the flight, David goes over and over the letter to make sure he hasn't missed anything of importance. At the same time, his father's diary is always on his mind. David still has not figured how or what he is going to do about his father's wishes.

CHAPTER 6

The plane lands. The bank has sent a car to pick David up and chauffeur him back to the bank, where he is greeted in the lobby by Christian Krobenberg. The two men shake hands then engage in normal small talk and pleasantries.

Christian tells David, "I would like to present you to our bank president, as a matter of normal protocol."

The three men join in a short conversation about each's home and families and then it is decided to get down to business.

Christian says to David, "On the phone, you gave me an account number which I verified as being a good number. All I need now is the document you have and a quick verification of the authenticity of the signature. If all is correct, then the account will become yours."

David pulls out the letter and hands it to Christian, who immediately hands it to their handwriting expert for verification. He takes the card and signature and then goes about verifying the signature with the signature card that has been on file at the bank.

"This will take a few minutes, Mr. Adelman. Would you like something to drink while we are waiting?"

"Yes, thanks," says David. "Right now, my mouth is like a desert. This anticipation is getting to me. Coffee would be fine."

Christian turns and gestures to the secretary in attendance to please fetch them both a cup of coffee. When she returns, she has two tiny little cups, and David is introduced to the European version of a cup of coffee.

Not only is the cup tiny, but what is in it is like molasses to David. He doesn't realize that they have brought him a cup of espresso. He tastes the espresso and decides he is not as thirsty as he thought.

Christian, being the shrewd person that he is, observes David's reaction to the coffee and intervenes. "I am so sorry, Mr. Adelman. You Americans brew your coffee a little different than we do on the continent."

With that, he sends the secretary back out, and she knows exactly what to do. Within just a moment, she returns with a coffee that David is more familiar with.

"Thank you," David says. "This is more my style."

In just a few more minutes, the handwriting expert arrives back at the screening room, hands the letter to Christian, and there, stamped on the letter, are the words *Confirmed as Correct*.

Christian turns to David, who has this gigantic smile on his face, and puts out his hand to shake it, then says, "We are pleased to house your account, Mr. Adelman."

David shakes his hand and a very big sigh of relief comes over him. "Damn it, I can't believe this is happening." Then he turns to Christian and asks, "Would it be possible to find out the value of the account at this time?"

"Why certainly, sir. How stupid of me not to have had this ready for you." Christian opens a file folder and begins to read aloud the line items listed on the tally sheet representing the Adelman estate.

After a very short moment, David interrupts him and asks, "Would it be possible, for now, just to get a total ball park number of the value of the estate?"

Christian looks at him and then looks at the bottom of the ledger sheet. "Now, you know this is not to the penny, as we still have some current entries that need to be calculated to make it current."

"Not a problem," David says.

"Sir, I am showing a current balance of about $496,000,000 in American dollars."

David is totally stunned and starts to collapse but is caught by the handwriting expert. He has turned white; the look on his face is one of total disbelief and amazement. He starts to talk, but nothing is coming out of his mouth. Finally, he stutters out, "D-d-d-did I hear you correct? I thought you just said about a half a billion dollars."

"Yes, sir, that is reasonably correct. But as I said, there are entries that need to be made yet, to get it current."

David looks at him and says, "Earlier, you said a reasonable amount. I would hate to see what you call a lot of money. Oh my God, gentlemen, I need to sit down for a few minutes. And I need to be alone as well. I have a phone call I have to make, then later we can go over the protocol that goes with this, and how we are going to manage the account."

They lead David to a very plush lounge, where he is told, "Use the bar as needed. Anything special you desire, just push the green button on the table and a secretary will come in to take care of your requests."

###

Back home in the States, the phone rings and Loraine says, "Hello?"

David says, "Hi, honey. Well, we now have few more dollars than we did last week."

"You're kidding. How did it go? How many more dollars do we have? Can I buy a new dishwasher?"

"How would you like to own a dishwasher manufacturing company?"

"Come on, David, stop it. What did you get?"

"Are you sitting down? If not, please sit down."

"Damn it, David! How much did you get?"

"Okay, you asked for it. Would you believe a half *billion* dollars?"

"No. Are you going to tell me the truth, or are you sleeping on the couch when you get home?"

David says, "You're right, that is high. Actually it is only $496,000,000, and that is the truth."

David has to take the phone from his ear, as all he can hear is Loraine screaming and screaming and screaming. She finally comes back to the phone and says, "If you are pulling my leg, I will never, ever talk to you again."

"I assure you, honey, it is real, and the paperwork is completed. It is ours. My dear, you are, as of today, one of the richest women in the country." Then, razzing her, David continues, "Looks like you're going to have to learn to be a socialite, go to tea parties, and then attend some of those fundraising dinners. Are you up to it?"

Loraine says, "I am sure someone is going to pinch me and all this is going to be a dream. I just know it is."

"No dream, babe. Now, I will need to spend a few days here to finalize what and how we are going to handle the account. But as soon as I get finished, I will be home. Love ya', babe."

David next sees Christian, and the two of them decide to meet the next morning to finalize David's account and set it up to meet his demands.

The next day, reality sets in, and David feels like he has his head screwed back on. He arrives at the bank then he and Christian sit at a conference table with stacks of papers all over the place that all deal with some aspect of David's new account.

David is amazed at how many different investment deals are in his portfolio.

"Tell me, Christian, how did this all come about? How did it grow to such proportions?"

"Well, actually, it was before my time. Or I should say most of it was before my time—I did have some effect on it. As I said earlier, Mr. Simon Berlinger was the person with whom your uncle met and who set up the account initially. It was agreed back then that your uncle's investments would be put in our investment branch, where they would execute all the necessary trades over the years. Needless to say, we have a very good investment branch, and they did extremely well with your uncle's assets. I guess the biggest asset was a small diamond company in which your uncle had a small part-ownership back in the late 1920s. You know them today as DeBeers, the largest diamond supplier in the world. Your uncle was a very shrewd man and had several other investments that, although they didn't grow as big and fast as DeBeers, did quite well in their own right, each one of them.

"All this, coupled with the investments that were made by the bank over the years, and your account has grown substantially. It is estimated that, if you were to continue your investments under our management, at the going rate your estate would, in ten years, double to over one billion dollars.

"That is why our account executives would like me to propose a business deal with you, Mr. Adelman. We would like to suggest that you leave the bulk of your estate in our bank, under our investment branch. We can set up any type of account management you desire, even have part of your estate transferred to the bank of your choice. One that, perhaps, is in the United States, which would make it much easier for you to facilitate withdrawals and make other business arrangements. I am sure you are going to be involved in your holdings. A man of your caliber will in all likelihood do quite well. Any assistance or guidance needed, we would be quite happy to assist."

Several hours pass and finally the two men come to an agreement as to how the estate will be handled. David agrees with Christian and the plan he lays out. It makes him comfortable and yet gives him access to all he will need.

David tells Christian, "There are a couple of loose ends that I would like to tie up before I leave. First, my own will and the continuance of the estate. I would like you to draw up the proper papers for my family to take over my total inheritance upon my death. In my uncle's will, he also asks us to take care of any of the relatives of his six buddies who were in prison with him. I plan to find them, if there are any out there. I will want them each receive to receive $2 million tax free. We will pay the tax on it."

"Not a problem, Mr. Adelman. I can assure you, your desires will be carried out to the letter," says Christian.

"I want to take this time to thank you and the bank and to state my total confidence in your decision making. Again, thank you sincerely."

CHAPTER 7

Upon arrival home, David and Loraine are beside themselves with happiness, as well as astonishment. They try to figure out what to do next, which is not as easy as one would think. A lot of decisions have to be made, and just getting started is tough enough. David assures Loraine that one of the first things he did was to make sure he has a will himself, so that the family is protected no matter what happens.

Once the excitement of the inheritance subsides, David turns his attention back to his father's diary. One thing that they are both excited about is the note attached to the bottom of the will by David's Uncle Ben, telling of the brutal rape and killing of David's mother and two sisters, and how David had been witness to the entire ordeal. Now, at long last, David has an answer to his nightmares. It all makes sense, and his memory starts to fall in place, as well. Hopefully, the nightmares will soon stop as a result, and they will be able to start a new part of their life.

One without all the pain and anger that has haunted David for twenty-five years.

In their quest for answers as to what to do next or how to handle the events that are opening up in their lives, they find themselves confused as to how to start. Finally they decide to do nothing for at least a week or two, in order to give them time to get their heads screwed back on.

"Thank God for the business degree I got in college," David says to Loraine. "At least I have a starting point and some idea as to how to go about this."

Both of them are in agreement that, without Dr. Flarity, they would not have anything, so they agree to give something to him, to show their appreciation.

The next day, both David and Loraine show up at Dr. Flarity's office and are greeted by the secretary. David says, "We would like to see the doctor, but we don't have an appointment."

In about three minutes, the doctor shows up and greets them, then asks them to join him in his office.

David starts to tell him about the diary and how they found the secret document that was hidden in the cover, then how this document led to their receiving the inheritance. Finally, David shares one final item with the doctor: the note at the bottom and what it described.

"I believe this is the root cause of my horrible dreams," he says.

"You know, David, I agree with you. Here is hoping it ends the dreams. Have you had any since the discovery of the note?"

David answers, "No, not yet, but it is still a little early. I do feel very comfortable about it. We are praying that this is the end of it."

About this time, David takes out a check and hands it to the doctor.

Dr. Flarity says, "This is not necessary" before even looking at the check. Then he studies it and realizes its size. "$200,000! My goodness, David, this is too much money."

"No it isn't, Doc. Not for everything you gave us. Without you and your attention to detail, we would not have anything, and the dreams would still be haunting us. Please accept this and our gratitude." David seems very pleased.

The Adelmans shake hands with the doctor and then leave.

As David walks out of the office, he turns and looks back one more time at the door knob. Then he smiles and says to Loraine, "Man, I feel good about that."

###

Three weeks after they last discussed what their future plans were going to be, David and Loraine sit down to lay out a game plan. Just what do they want? Well, obviously, a new house is in the cards. But with David still being in the military, a new house doesn't make sense, not so long as there is a chance they may be transferred to another base. Until they stop traveling, a house will simply be an item on their wish list.

David says, "The first thing I am going to do is hire my old college buddy, Rob Preston. You remember him, don't you, honey?"

Loraine says, "Sure. He is the guy who went on to become a very successful lawyer."

"That's correct. Besides being a good lawyer, he is someone I can trust. I will contact him this week and see if he will come on board with us to help manage our financial accounts and give me guidance with our business dealings in the future. At least the ones that are here in the States. I think I am going to hang up the swim flippers and retire from the Navy. With the vast fortune we are responsible for, I don't need to get deployed to Afghanistan and get my head shot off."

Loraine is very understanding. "I know you will miss the active life, honey, but I agree with you.

Whatever it takes to keep you with me and the kids, I am game for."

Life makes a 180-degree turn for David. He becomes a businessman trying to survive in the world of business and starts to find new activities to take up his time. A new awareness of life comes over him.

I would like to say that all is well with David, but it is not. The dreams seem to have stopped, but he harbors a feeling of uneasiness and wrestles with what he thinks it may mean. He constantly thinks about the diary and the fact that it was actually a wish list. David remembers telling his friend and fellow Navy SEAL, Finney, how it would cost a fortune to find all those men and then deal with bringing them to justice. Well, now he suddenly has the fortune but wonders does he have the will and desire to follow up on his father's wishes?

A new haunting starts to take root in David. His father is reaching out from the grave, pulling at him. The diary is like a magnet: it keeps drawing David back to it and to his father's wishes.

Finally David decides to at least reach out and see if any of this is possible. He asks his buddy Rob Preston to find him the top investigating company in the country.

After about a week, Rob calls him and says, "I've set up a phone meeting between you and the president of SSI, Search & Seizure, Inc. The owner and president is a guy by the name of Duke Rutlege."

It isn't long before Mr. Rutlege calls David and asks, "What can I do for you, Mr. Adelman?"

"I would like to meet face to face on this matter," David explains. "Are you available tomorrow at noon, at the café of the Green Dragon on South Street?"

"Sure, no problem. I will be there at noon."

###

As David sits enjoying his morning coffee at the Green Dragon, 11:58 AM comes and goes, but there is no sign of Duke Rutlege. This does not sit well with David, as he has come to expect people to be prompt. As the chimes on the bell tower across the street chime noon, however, Mr. Rutlege sits down next to David.

David is shocked. He turns to say, "Hello," just as Rutlege puts out his hand to greet him. They shake hands and go through the normal small talk that usually takes place between strangers as they jockey for position. Each tries to get an edge on the other person.

Rutlege is a smooth looking character, one who looks like he knows what you're going to sa, before you say it. There is an air about him that reeks of efficiency. Nothing on him is out of place. Everything is just so, which almost reminds David of a military man. David senses this and is impressed with it. He feels this is the type of guy who just might be able to carry out this exercise, if anyone can.

"Say, Mr. Rutlege," David begins, breaking the ice.

"Please, my name is Duke. Mr. Rutlege, my father, died several years ago. Besides, I like my conversation to be informal, I can get much more done that way, and it gives me a better feel for the character of the person I am talking to."

"Fine, Duke. I get this feeling you might be ex-ops," says David.

"You're very astute, Mr. Adelman. Green berets, actually. Twenty-two years."

"Welcome to the club. Navy SEALs, eleven years," David answers back.

Duke looks at him and says jokingly, "It's a shame we don't have some kind of special brotherhood, secret-club handshake."

David laughs and then Duke laughs, too. It's obvious both these two guys are bad asses, each in their own right. So, for either of them to try and get an edge on the other is not going to happen.

David leans over and says, "I like you, Duke, so let me put a business offer on the table for you. I will even sweeten the pot a little more than I had planned, one bad ass to another."

Duke comes back at him, "Hey, guy, my day is yours."

David begins to lay out the story. "My father was a prisoner in the Holocaust and died in Dachau Prison. He kept a list of names of the really bad of the bad, when it came to the SS guards. He even listed the atrocities that each was guilty of committing. These men were no good, scum of the earth people who would just as soon kill you as look at you."

"I'm aware of them and their bad-ass reputation," states Duke.

David continues, "It was my father's wish that sometime in the future these horrible men would meet their just end. The list of names comes to fifteen, and after each is a list of addresses and any other info that might help in locating these men after the war. I am asking you to track these men down, find out where they live today and under what name. Some may already be dead for any number of reasons.

"Duke, for each person you are successful in finding, I will pay you $25,000, and if you find or locate all fifteen, I will give you a bonus of $100,000. If you do this within six months, I will give you an extra $100,000. Let me make myself clear, I need accurate info including pictures of them as they look today. If they have family members, I need to know who and how many, but nothing more on the family members." David leans over really close to him, stares him right in the eye, and asks, "Are you good enough for this?"

"Mr. Adelman, if I can't do it, no one can. We have a deal."

The two men stand up, shake hands to close the deal, and then start to part company.

David says to Duke, "How would you like to make another $100,000?"

Duke looks at him and says, "Okay, who do I have to kill for it?"

David laughs heartily. "While in prison, my father befriended about six men, and all six died together in prison. My father wanted to give some money to any of his friend's family members, if they survived the war. I have the list of the six men and their information. I'm trying to find any of their living heirs today. I will be surprised if you can find any of them, but if you give me an honest try, then I will give you the hundred thousand anyway."

Again they shake hands, and Duke says, "Deal."

"By the way," says David, "I have your business card, so I will send you the list of names and the information that I have on each. I am also going to include a check for fifty thousand as upfront money. It will help you on expenses."

Their meeting concluded, the men part company, and David heads back for home.

CHAPTER 8

Time moves on, and David continues to become more and more of a businessman, dealing with investments and constantly looking for other business deals to get involved in. The hiring of his friend Rob Preston is turning out to be a smart move on David's part. Rob is able to take a lot of the business pressure off of David and allow him to adjust to his new world. Since his involvement with SSI, David takes on a new air about himself. He knows his father wanted this done, and at least for now, David has started the ball rolling. Where this takes him, he does not know for certain. He is not sure just how far he will allow this go, but for now, he is in control of it.

David imagines it will be interesting once Rutlege delivers to him a report of all of the information he's gathered. At that point, he will have to decide just what he wants to do next. David knows this moment is coming; he can feel his emotions build, as time passes. The dream/nightmares seem to have subsided but not disappeared completely. Instead of the sweat treatment and the screams, David has begun to feel guilt, as though he is not full fulfilling his father's desires. His deceased father is beginning to demand a bigger and bigger part in David's life.

Five months after David's initial meeting with Rutlege of SSI, suddenly he receives an envelope in the mail. Upon opening it, he sees an update on exactly where Rutlege is with his assignment, as of that moment in time. Upon examination of the material, it is obvious that SSI is very good at their job. Rutlege has found most of the candidates David requested, but there are still a few left to be located.

As for the relatives of the friends of his father's, he has completed the hunt and is sorry to report that there is only one person connected with the list of friends who is still alive.

That person is a woman who lives in England, and her maiden name was Berkowitz. Denise Berkowitz currently lives at 153 North Yorkshire Drive outside of London, and her phone number is (020) 7222-2978. This makes David feel good. He knows he is fulfilling his Uncle's desires, along with what he is sure would have been his father's, as well.

Upon receiving this information, David contacts his friend Rob Preston and asks him to go to

England to reach out to this lady so that they can give her 2 million British pounds (or about $3,078,400 in U.S. dollars). He must make sure this gift it tax free.

David tells Rob, "Please give it to her in cash in an attaché case. I do not want her to know who gave it to her, only why—that her father was the friend of this wealthy Jew in Dachau and they died together."

Rob accepts the assignment and says he can leave in a couple of days.

###

Once Rob is able to get on his way, within twelve hours he is in England. From his hotel room, he contacts Ms. Berkowitz and explains, "I have something of value that needs to be presented to you, and to you only. This goes back to the time your father was in Dachau Prison."

The two of them agree upon a time and place.

Rob shows up at his appointed time to meet with Ms. Berkowitz and presses the door buzzer. The door opens, and a woman in her late thirties is standing in front of Rob. She is not a stunning lady, but not totally unattractive either.

"Yes, what can I do for you?" she asks.

Rob says, "I am the gentleman with whom you talked on the phone a few hours ago, and this is about your father, Solomon Berkowitz."

She greets him and invites Rob to come inside then offers him a traditional cup of tea, which Rob happily accepts.

Once the formalities are covered, Rob presents her his business card. This is when she realizes that he is a lawyer representing a client.

"My Name is Ronald Preston, attorney at law. I am afraid that is all I can tell you about who I am or represent. I am not allowed to go any further on those details. During, the war, however, your father Solomon befriended a person of interest, represented by my client. Your father and this other prisoner became very close friends during the year they were in Dachau. Needless to say, they suffered together, and they died there together. One of them left a will, and that will has just recently come to light. My client has entrusted me to give you this attaché case with its contents, and to tell you that the money is clear—all taxes have been paid on it—so you may do as you wish with the entire amount."

Rob hands Ms. Berkowitz the case, and she commences to open it. The contents revealed are shocking to her. She can't believe what she sees! She seems to be in a state of shock, just staring at the open case, her eyes as big as saucers.

Rob asks, "Are you alright, madam?"

"Yes, yes, I just can't believe this. About three hours ago, I was trying to budget my finances and juggle my accounts so I could have my car repaired. Now I have more money than I ever dreamed of."

Rob tells her, "I assure you, it is real. The total amount is two million British pounds. It's all yours. Having completed my business here, I will be leaving. My client and I wish you much success with the money. May it bring you all that you would dream for, along with much happiness."

Ms. Berkowitz says, "Thank you so very much. I am at a loss for words to express my gratitude. My husband is going to go bananas. Maybe now he can retire from his policeman's job."

Denise Berkowitz gives Rob a peck on the cheek and thanks him again.

On his way back to the U.S., Rob calls David to tell him how things went. "She got the money and was ecstatic at the gift. She and her husband live in a modest house, so it would appear they will be able to use the money.

"She mentioned that her husband was in law enforcement, so I got the impression that this may enable him to retire at a decent age. All and all, David, this was a very good thing you have done. I should be back by sometime tomorrow morning. See you then, buddy. Save a cold one for me."

"Thanks, Rob. See you then," says David.

By this time, David has become more and more worried about his feelings of guilt pertaining to his father's wish list. The knowledge of how and where his mother and two sisters died is also beginning to add his resentment toward the named list of Nazi guards.

When the six months are up, right on cue, Duke Rutlege contacts David to give him his final report along with the list of information that David wanted.

They meet again at the Green Dragon, and Duke hands David a very thick file folder with all the information he requested.

"Well," David ask, "did you find them all?"

"Yes, sir. Every last one of the bastards. Of course, some are already in the ground. You see, two of them were killed during the very end of the war by American soldiers.

"One committed suicide after the war, a Felix Mayer. I guess his conscience got the best of him, so he took a nine millimeter pistol to the head. One Dolf Schulz died just a few years ago. He was driving a sports car and decided to take this turn too fast, and into the wild blue yonder he went. The stop at the bottom of the ravine is what killed him. These guys are currently located all over the world, but I think three, maybe four, are in the U.S."

"Duke, you did great job. I am impressed with your efficiency and quickness," says David. "I can almost guarantee you we will do more business in the future. Your check will be in the mail tomorrow, or, if you wish, I can have my lawyer deliver it to you in person tomorrow."

"Not a problem, Mr. Adelman. The mail is fine."

David takes the list of names and locations and heads for home. Upon arriving there, he grabs a beer from the fridge then plops down in his favorite TV chair and starts to study the file given to him by Duke. He is right: these guys are all over the world. But a bigger question is forming in David's mind: *what am I going to do about them?*

David's father is in his head, talking to him again. This coupled with his growing anger about the fates of his mother and sisters, really starts to take a toll on David. Now that he has all the information needed to locate the perpetrators, as well as the fortune to support it, it is time for him to make some hardball decisions as to what he is going to do next.

David continues to struggle with an answer to this last question; at the same time, his guilt grows stronger and stronger.

He suffers through many sleepless nights over the next few weeks, trying to arrive at a final decision. Should he turn them over to the law? Or should he obey his father's wishes and exterminate them himself? Not easy questions to answer.

This idea of killing these men is not really the big question; they need to die and would die, if they were ever caught by the authorities. They would be tried as war criminals and executed; the criminals know that. The problem David faces is should he do it? If not him, chances are that none of them will get their just punishment.

In his mind, David tries to envision himself as an executioner and not as a murderer. This killing of people is not new to David; that is exactly what he is—a professional killer, trained by the U.S. Navy, and very good at his job. His problem, however, is in justifying the death of each man. On one side, David knows they deserve to die, as war criminals and butchers. On the other hand, he has this wish list of his father's that is asking him to kill these men in an attempt to exact retribution.

David continues to face the vision of seeing his mother and two sisters killed in front of him. As this thought process begins to take shape, it pushes him toward being the executioner. He has killed people in the past, but never as a premeditated kill. The deaths have always been in the line of duty or, as they say in the military, the mission. He is good at it and has even done it up close and very personal, with a knife.

The bad thing about all this is that he has no one he can confide in, to try and balance his thoughts. He doesn't dare tell his wife: she and most people would consider this an act of murder, and to many, it would be *mass murder*. He doesn't dare tell any of his friends or military contacts, either, for fear they might someday get questioned about the killings and accidently spill the beans on what David once discussed with them.

Finally, David makes the hardball decision. The dreams of his father along with remembering his mother and sisters become enough to push him over the edge.

He begins to plan and prepare for the killings of these former SS guards by his own hand. This is not something he has decided lightly. He is well aware that, if he were to get caught, he might very well go to the electric chair and his family will be in shame for the rest of their lives. If it's found out, no one will care that he was doing it to see justice done.

David spends several days giving this decision some more thought. Just what does he plan to do, and how does he plan to do it? Is there a timeframe attached to it? Is he going to hurry to get it done or take his sweet time? There are so many things to think about, and each one impacts David's thinking.

Since receiving the inheritance, David has found himself doing a considerable amount of traveling. So, if he has to travel to a specific town or country, he can easily make it appear to be a normal business trip. He decides that this will be the way for him to set up his alibi from time to time. In addition, money is certainly no problem; it should buy him considerable leverage in his hunt and travels.

When it is finally time for him to begin, David looks at the first name on his list. It is someone who lives in Chicago. David decides that this is going to work out fine for him, as he already has a business meeting planned in Chicago.

As David packs for the business trip, Loraine asks, "Where are you going this time?"

"Have to be in Chicago by tomorrow. But I don't expect it to take me more than a day, maybe three at the most."

The meeting is only about three hours long, but he is not comfortable yet with how he plans to carry out these killings, so he wants to leave himself plenty of time to get the lay of the land, especially on the first one.

David decides to take a tranquilizing dart gun with him, in case he should run into a dog or in the event that a family member stumbles in on the killing. The dart gun will allow him to put down any intruder without hurting them. David has decided that he and his family have no judgments against any of the family members of the men on the list, so he wants to do all he can to protect them.

He is off to Chicago and quickly takes care of the regular business for which the trip was intended. Next he starts to case the neighborhood where the suspect lives.

It is not in a high-rent district. Quite frankly, there are not a lot of people milling around at the time of night David arrives. In fact, with all the murders that already often take place in this neighborhood, David doesn't think he will appear out of place. He thinks about the job at hand and is grateful for the Navy training that taught him how to move and not be seen or heard.

David stands in the shadows, watching his target walk down the street toward him. His plan is to walk by him and pull him into the alley and then thrust a knife into his heart. As he starts his walk to meet up with the man, David's own heart is pumping faster and faster until he is standing next to the man. Then David puts his hand over the man's mouth so he cannot scream and drags him into the alley. Just as he is about to drive the knife home, he senses he is having second thoughts, and so he backs off the man.

The man yells at David, "What the hell are you doing, you son of a bitch?"

David is at a loss for words and starts shaking, not knowing if he wants to do this or not. He looks at the man and simply says, "Dachau Prison."

The man turns white and realizes instantly that he is facing what he's known would come someday. He yells at David, "You Jew bastard."

This startles David, and he lunges forward, driving the knife deep into the man's heart. He is so upset with the man for yelling what he did, he decides to take the knife and carve a small Star of David in the man's forehead.

Within twenty-four hours, David is back home. He tells Loraine, "Things went easier than planned. Didn't have any trouble at all. As a matter of fact, you could say the client was dying to close the deal, it went that smoothly."

If by chance you had read the *Chicago Tribune* the next day, you would have seen an article that talked about a middle-aged man by the name of Albert Muller who was killed in an alley with a knife wound to the heart.

The article would go on to say, *It must have been some kind of gang murder, because the dead man had a Star cut into his forehead with a knife.*

Some will say, "It looked like the Star of David, the Jewish symbol." But given the numbers of murders in Chicago in any given year, no one gives it much attention. It's just another murder.

As David sits drinking his beer at home in his favorite chair, he gets a big smile on his face. *This was easier than expected*, he thinks. *Things went like clockwork. Who is going to be next?*

Some three weeks later, David finds he has to be in Los Angeles to discuss a business deal with a national brand distributor he is interested in dealing with. Upon checking his list, he sees that one of the men on the list is also located in Los Angeles. He decides this is a good time to kill two birds with one stone, so to speak. So he headed off for Los Angeles.

When he arrives, David rents a car and goes about meeting with this business client, closing the deal. Pleased that his timeframe is working well for him, David next checks out the name on his list.

The guy's name is Bjorn Schmidt. David finds Schmidt's address and spends the next night parked down the street from his house, getting a feel for the local traffic and the habits of his target. This time, David will not be working on the slum side of town, so a little more care will be appropriate. He has his stun gun with him, just in case.

He is in luck again. Schmidt is a bachelor and lives alone. By 8:00 PM, his target is alone in the house and appears to be deep into television. David cases the house very thoroughly, and by 8:15 is in the house, standing in the hall, watching him as he drinks his beer and pets his dog.

The dog is a big German Shepherd and not one to mess with. David is aware he will have to deal with the dog first, lest it attack him. It is hard to tell how this will come out. While he hides out of view of Schmidt and the dog, he can see everything that is happening. His idea is to walk into the room, startle the dog so it sits up right then quickly dart the dog to immobilize it. At that point, he will be able to deal with Schmidt.

Once David feels comfortable that all is well, he steps into full view of Schmidt. Schmidt is startled, and, as planned, the dog sits upright in full view. *Zap*! David has the dog taken care of.

Schmidt starts to jump up, but David shows his 9mm Beretta and tells him, "Sit back down."

The man yells, "What do you want? I don't have much money, but you can have all I go. Just let me alone."

David asks, "What is your name?"

He answers, "Jeremy Jacobs."

"Herr Bjorn Schmidt, you mean. You don't even remember your name. Do you remember Dachau?" asks David

At this time, Schmidt says, "Oh my God, it's finally come."

David then ties him to a chair and, after reminding him of all the people he tortured at Dachau then slips a plastic bag over Schmidt's head.

As Schmidt begins to suffocate, David keeps talking to him. "Remember the prison and the terrible things you did to those poor, helpless people? This is the price you must pay for those deeds. I trust all those people you killed are passing in review for you."

In just a few minutes he is dead from suffocation. David removes the bag then takes out his knife and begins to carve the Star of David in his forehead. Then he places the bag back over his head.

David can't help himself: he checks on the dog to make sure it is breathing properly and will recover soon. He then quietly exits the house through the back door and slips away into the night.

His work is done, so he prepare for his trip back home. When he finally arrives at his house, he greets the kids and gives them toys he bought for them in Los Angeles.

The next day, a small article appears in the paper making note of a murder that previous night. The article tells how a ruthless killer murdered middle-aged Jeremy Jacobs in his own home by putting a plastic bag over his head, causing him to suffocate to death. The article goes on to say it must have been another gang murder, as the gang carved a Star in the man's forehead, presumably as a calling card. No witnesses or clues were found. One thing that is taken as odd is that the man had a large German Shepherd dog on the premises.

The next day, one of the guys at David's office asks, "How the business deal went?"

David says, "It was a good trip. The customer he contacted. He was breathless about my presentation."

Things continue to go very smoothly for David and his business connections. There are hiccups here and there, but that is always to be expected in business. Life at home stays great; Loraine starts having the time of her life, adjusting to her new style of living.

About a month later, a deal is being put together that will require David to visit London. He is tempted to visit the Berkowitz woman, to see how she is handling the sudden large inheritance, but he feels it best he leave that alone.

Upon checking his hit list, however, he confirms that an August Schroder is still living in London. So David prepares to do his usual thing while there. Going out of the country, however, means David will have to leave his dart pistol at home. It simply will not pass through the new metal detectors recently installed at all U.S. airports. This fact makes him a little nervous, so he hopes he won't need it.

The trip is pleasant, and most of what he has to do gets done relatively quickly, which leaves him with extra time to spare in London. The first thing that David does is to case the house where Schroder lives. He sees he has a wife who lives with him, but also notices that she goes out each afternoon for about three hours to do whatever she does, and then returns home at a regular time.

David positions himself for a quick entry once Schroder's wife leaves. When she has left the house, David quietly slips in through a cellar door and then climbs up the steps to the kitchen. Once there, he pulls out a 9mm pistol that he was able to buy earlier that day and then screws on the silencer he bought in London, as well.

Schroder is sitting in his living room when he thinks he hears something in the kitchen.

He gets up and walks to the kitchen. When he turns the corner to the kitchen, he finds himself eyeball to eyeball with David.

Being middle-aged, he is no match for David and his masculine physique. David gives him a right upper cut with his fist that puts Schroder on the floor instantly. He then drags Schroder over to the kitchen table, where he ties him up with the rope he has brought with him.

David says, "All right, big guy, let's you and me talk a little."

Schroder looks at him and barks, "What the hell do you want, you scum bag?"

"Let me ask you a simple question to start, and I must warn you, the correct answers are important. What is your name?"

Schroder answers, "None of your damn business."

With that answer, David takes his pistol and puts one bullet in Schroder's left leg. Schroder screams and jerks violently in pain. "We will try that one more time, until you figure out how to play the game. What is your name?"

"George Caraway."

"Are you sure?" asks David.

"Yes, I know my own name."

This time, David puts a bullet in his right leg and watches as he screams again with pain.

"Let's try it again, and this time I will help you. What is your Dachau name?"

With that comment, Schroder knows what he is really up against and fires back at David, "Are you one of those filthy Jews?"

"Wrong thing to say, dumb ass."

This time, David puts a bullet in Schroder's left arm, and the pain has to be staggering by this time. With three shots in him, he is trying his best to stay conscious.

"All right. My name is August Schroder."

David says, "Now you are catching on."

Schroder looks at him and says, "All you Jews should have been exterminated,"

With that, David puts another bullet in his other arm. By this time, Schroder has passed out. David takes his knife out and, while Schroder is passed out, carves the Star on his forehead. Then he gets a pitcher of water to toss on him in an attempt to revive him. After David pours the water on him Schroder begins to revive, and a semblance of awareness comes over him as blood runs down into his face from the cuts in his forehead.

David looks at him and says, "I wanted you to be awake. I want you to know why this is taking place. I want you to know all those people you tortured in Dachau are getting payback. And most importantly, I want you to see this." And with that, David points the gun at Schroder's head and just stands there for a few minutes, giving Schroder time to contemplate what is about to happen. Then David puts a bullet right in the middle of his forehead.

David turns, looks around the room to make sure he has not left anything, and then walks out the back door and down the alley. As he passes the river, he tosses the 9mm into the water with the silencer still attached. He then tosses in the knife he used, after wiping it clean.

With his business in London completed, David catches the first available flight home.

Upon reaching home, Loraine asks, "How was the trip? Did you close the deal?"

"It was okay, but there were a lot of holes in the deal. I was able to complete it anyway, though. But you know, honey, some guys are just hard learners. Finally I was able to convince him of my wisdom, though," says David.

Obviously, the next day, in the *London Daily*, there is an article about a murder of a middle-aged man by the name of George Caraway. The article tries to explore how or even why this murder may have taken place, but they really don't do too good of a job, other than to say, *It was a brutal murder where the victim was shot five times, once in each extremity and then in the forehead, where the killer had carved the Star of David in his forehead skin.*"

CHAPTER 9

Normally, this murder would go **unnoticed** by Scotland Yard, but some agent realizes that this crime is extremely unusual and decides to put the killing on the international wire service to see if anything pops up. A few hours later, an inspector is checking the wire service and sees a report from the U.S.

It says, *In regards to killings or murders and in particular those that have the victims with the Star of David carved in their forehead, we have had two cases here in the U.S. within the last two months. Both have been unusual killings in that one involved a knife put in the victim's heart and the other involved a plastic bag placed over the victim's head, forcing him to suffocate to death. Both had a Star carved into the forehead.*

The inspector looks at the report and says, "Bingo. We have a serial killer on our hands."

Chief Inspector Casey calls in Inspector Saun Torrey and shows him the story that is developing.

"I want you to contact the FBI in Washington and make a connection to let them know what we have on this case to date. See if they are interested in putting a joint team on this."

Inspector Torrey makes the contact and is surprised when he receives word back that they are very interested in a joint effort on this project.

The chief says, "Good. I am going to send you to the States for a little bit to see how this breaks and what direction it takes. I have a strange feeling about this case. This Star of David on the forehead is not good. I am going to release you from the Yard for two months, so if you see it taking longer then let me know. I'll see how we want to go from there. But keep me posted."

"Will do, Chief," says Saun.

Saun goes home and breaks the news to his wife Denise. "I am going out of the country for a while. Not sure how long, but the chief has released me for up to sixty days."

"You will take care, won't you?" she says.

"Of course, love."

Inspector Torrey travels to the U.S. and is greeted at the airport by a driver from FBI headquarters. "Good afternoon, Inspector. Did you have a good comfortable trip?" asks the driver.

"Yes, it wasn't too bad. We hit some air but overall, it was okay."

He gets into the car and they are off. About thirty minutes and a whole bunch of small talk later, they arrive at the FBI main headquarters, where he is met by the head of the division. They greet each other and exchange pleasantries, then they meet in a board room in order to lay out the case and see how best to pursue it. Assigned to the case representing the FBI is inspector Rob Stevens, a fifteen-year veteran of the department and one hell of a nice guy.

Rob is introduced to Saun from Scotland Yard. The two shake hands and greet each other. As the two inspectors talk to each other, it is apparent that they are going to get along very nicely together. They communicate with each other for no more than ten minutes before the two already seem to be enjoying the other's company. This kind of a situation almost always makes the case a little easier to handle.

Rob tells Saun, "Since you are going to be here for a while, let's get you a place to stay and let you settle in. Then we can have dinner this evening and talk a little about the case, just to familiarize ourselves."

Saun says to Rob, "Sounds like a plan."

Then the two are off in Rob's car to a local hotel that the FBI uses quite often in cases like this.

After Saun gets checked in and has time to freshen up, Rob picks him up and off to dinner they go. The evening is a typical summer evening, and Saun is already enjoying his trip to the States. A couple of mixed drinks later, the two start to discuss the case. They agree that this is going to become very interesting before it is over.

Saun asks Rob, "What is your impression of the facts, as we know them at this early point?"

Rob says, "The Star of David is the outstanding fact in the case right now. The style of murders, although cruel and unusual, are not that outstanding in their application. The Star of David is the one item that is really unusual. Let me ask you Saun, when you think of the Star of David, what do you think of?"

"Why, the Jewish community."

"Exactly."

"Now let me ask you that same question, only this time I want you to tie it to the murders. And since we have multiple murders, add mass murder to the list," says Rob.

"That's easy—the Holocaust."

"Correct, again," says Rob. "I think this case has something to do with the Holocaust, but what? That is the big question. The next question is, is it tied to the Holocaust in general, encompassing all Jews? Or is it tied to a particular place or event, maybe even one particular group?" asks Rob.

"You make a good point, Rob."

Rob continues, "I have been giving it some thought also, and I am wondering if we are chasing a person or a group. Usually, when a group commits retribution crimes, and we aren't sure these are retribution crimes yet, but anyway, when they do, they usually take responsibility for it. This is their way of saying to the world, 'we are here to be feared.' So far, I know of no one who has spoken up and said, 'here we are, look at what we can do.'"

"That's right. This is going to be one wild ride before it is over. Can't argue with you there, partner."

Once dinner is over and they have exhausted their information, they decide to call it a night.

Back at David's house, the family is still enjoying their new life and its luxuries. Now that David is no longer in the military, they have bought a new house and David is certainly enjoying his new, bright red Corvette. Loraine is the anchor here, so it is she who will keep everyone in line while they adjust to this new style of life.

David is still having his dream problems, but they are a little more varied now. It's almost as if he is being led into something. If David believed in the supernatural, he would probably say his dreams are telling him what to do; his father is the overriding character in them. It seems to him like his father and the list of names are taking over his dreams.

One of the names on his list is a Dirk Koch. He is living in Argentina. David has a trip planned for Brazil, but is also planning to visit Argentina to take care of some more of his father's business.

By the time comes for David to make his trip to South America, he has completed all the planning needed. He gives his family the usual kisses and hugs and is off for the airport.

The first stop is Brazil, where David goes to deal with a client he hopes will come on board with his import/export business. The meeting is relatively short, so afterwards David hops a transport and heads for Buenos Aires, Argentina.

Upon arrival in Buenos Aires, he finds himself a guide who can show him around the city, and after getting a good feel for the layout of the city, he then rents a car. Once he has acclimated himself to the city, David searches out the address of the man who is known as Raual Mendoza.

Mendoza lives in a modest house on the outskirts of town. David parks his car nearby and acts like a tourist taking pictures while at the same time focusing on Mendoza's house.

He notices that Mendoza leaves the house, the, walks down toward the valley for about two miles each afternoon, just passing the Del Cabrera café. The next day, David buys a roll of plastic and two hunting knifes. He covers the front seat of the rental car with the plastic, tucking it in so as to make it look like the car seat cover.

David is parked outside Mendoza's house at about 2:00 PM as he watches Mendoza leave the house, just like clockwork, and start his walk. He gives him about fifteen minutes to get some distance from the house, then David starts the car and begins to track Mendoza. This stretch of road has very little if any traffic on it, so it is a natural for David to make his approach and not be seen.

He drives down the road and then comes up alongside Mendoza and stops,

"Senor," he says, getting Mendoza's attention,

"Yes?

"Senor, can you tell me where the Café Del Cabrera is? I have an appointment, and I am going to be late," David states.

"Sure. I am going right past it, so I will show you the way." Mendoza opens the car door and gets in.

David starts out and within about two minutes pulls off the road into a small pull-off area. Before Mendoza can say or do anything, David has a knife at his throat.

"I suggest you sit very still or you will feel steel sooner than you want, Mr. Mendoza. I am going to ask you your name. I suggest you think very hard. before you answer... What is your name, your Dachau name?" asks David.

With that statement, Mendoza's eyes get very large and he realizes instantly what he is up against.

Mendoza asks, "Are you with the Israelis? The Mossad?"

"No, but you will wish I was before this is over. When you were a guard, you had no heart in your dealing with the prisoners of Dachau, so I plan to relieve you of yours."

With that, David thrusts the knife into Mendoza's chest. He then wraps him up in the car's plastic seat cover and drags his body out of the car and into the bushes. A few minutes later, David is tossing the knife and Mendoza's heart into the bushes while leaving his own calling card on Mendoza's forehead.

David then drives back to town. He checks the car over to make sure he isn't leaving anything incriminating behind, then returns it to the car rental and thanks the man.

He said, "I had a great time touring the city."

Back on the airplane heading home, he goes back over the events of the day, and then gets a big grin on his face. He is very happy with how things went for the trip. He thinks about his father for a moment, and then says to himself,

"Did I do good, today Father?"

Once David arrives back home, and the usual greetings of daddy and husband take place. Loraine asks, "How did the deal go?"

David tells her, "The guy really didn't have his heart in the deal, but he was able to close the deal anyway."

###

About two days later, Rob and Saun are reading the "pull off" sheet of the wire service. They are reading how a man was found in Buenos Aires who had been murdered, but it was a case of sadists committing murder or possibly some kind of gang revenge. The police had not ruled out drugs as the possible reason for the murder. It appears the man's heart was cut out, and a Star carved into his forehead. The man's name was Raul Mendoza.

Rob looks at Saun then says, "Well, I think we have one more clue to our case. I really do not believe these are the doings of an average John Doe, who may be killing for revenge. These killings are all over the globe, so it is going to take someone who has financial backing to simply do all this traveling and make these connections.

"We could have an organization involved or just a wealthy individual, but it definitely costs a lot of money to pull this off as efficiently as they have so far. This guy being in Argentina is where a lot of the Nazis went after the war. Do you suppose the Israeli Mossad is behind this?"

Saun says, "I don't know. It's their kind of work, with the exception of the forehead marking we've observed. I will contact my office and have them get ahold of our contact with the Mossad, to see if they will or can shed any light on it."

Rob says, "Great. I sure hope they can shed something on this. They just might be able to give us some direction, if nothing else."

That afternoon, Saun walks into Rob's office and says, "Got my return from headquarters. The Mossad reports that they are aware of the killings but are not the ones doing it. They also said that whoever it is certainly has their blessing. Each time a new murder goes up on the board, everyone in their office cheers. He did say one thing of interest that we pretty much already knew. The names being listed are aliases for Nazi war-crime criminals. It turns out whoever is doing this is saving the World War Crimes Agency a lot of time and money."

Although the Israelis are not losing any sleep over the killings, the attention of the law enforcement community around the world keeps a watchful eye on the situation. Quite frankly, there seems to be a hero effect starting to build around the murders. Everyone knows who and why the killings are happening. Who is going to worry about the world losing a bunch of really bad guys who deserve what they are getting, anyway?

As in any news story, the press jumps on these events and has dubbed the killer the "Revengeful Murderer." It is this kind of window dressing that sells newspapers. It isn't too long after the Argentina murder when two more murders pop up on the news wire. *The "Revengeful Murderer" strikes again.*

Again the newspaper tries to juice up the story: *In the still of night, the "Revengeful Murderer" has struck again, claiming two more war-crime criminals and ridding the earth of two more pieces of scum.*

The news media continues to have a ball with these new murders, one in Bavaria and another in France.

At the same time, every Nazi in hiding all over the world goes deeper into hiding and tries to cover their tracks. At the same time, they really begin to worry for their lives. Each one fears he may be next. David has caused panic among this group of people and is enjoying every moment of it.

Rob and Saun remain on the job but really don't have much to show for it. They do have to admit that their own desire to catch this vicious killer is waning, now that they have figured out what he is doing and especially to whom he is doing it. But their job dictates that they find him and bring him to justice. They both agree that the world can't condone vigilantes going on the rampage whenever and wherever they choose.

Rob suggests, "Saun, why don't you contact the Mossad again, and see if they can identify any of the men killed, and where the connection between all of them might be. Just what is the common denominator in all these killings? If we can find this out, we might be able to jump ahead of the killer and catch him in the act."

Saun agrees and makes the call back to his headquarters to relay their question.

CHAPTER 10

David and Loraine are enjoying life to the fullest. They have even bought a boat and spend a lot of their spare time relaxing on it. It is a twenty-six footer.

David falls into the regimen of a business tycoon and becomes a master at it. His college business degree begins to reap dividends for him.

One relaxing afternoon, he, Finney, and Rob Preston are enjoying themselves on the boat, having a few beers, and taking in some sun rays. Fishing poles hang over the edge. It is not clear whether the lines on their poles even have fish hooks on them, but it is all part of their ritual of relaxation.

At some point, Finney asks, "Hey, guys, have any of you been following the 'Revengeful Murderer' case that has been in the news?"

Boy, does this catch David by surprise.

"I haven't. Have you, Rob?" asks David

"A little. I really have to admire this guy. He is doing what the law enforcement community has been unable to do for the last twenty-five years. I am not sure I agree with the idea of being a vigilante, but with our sick society today, maybe that is what we need more of."

Of course, David is sitting back, taking this all in. Then he begins to grin from ear to ear. He thinks to himself, *If they only knew.*

Finney looks at David and asks "What are you grinning about, boss man?"

"Well, I was just wondering, if they ever catch this guy, what do you think they would do to him?"

Finney blurts out, "Pin a medal on him and parade him down 5th Avenue in New York."

"Naw, our laws don't work that way." Rob says. "We can't have people going around killing others just based on their own desire to do what they think is good. We are a country of laws, and we need to live by them."

"Spoken like a true lawyer," says Finney.

This conversation hits home with David and makes him begin to think. He starts to wrestle with the morality of what he is doing, not just what he thinks is the justice *behind* it.

It isn't too long after this that David goes to visit his Rabbi. He sits down with Rabbi Ahudi and discusses the idea of revenge: how one might be able to show a reason for it, but yet it leaves a feeling of guilt. So what is the correct path to take?

David uses the Holocaust as an example for applying revenge. He knows the killings are wrong, but he has so much guilt placed upon him that he feels this is his destiny, to fulfill his father's wishes so that so many millions of souls can be set free. He realizes that this issue is much bigger than just one man. He feels that millions are depending upon him.

The one consolation that he has is, right or wrong, at least world opinion is on his side. David never does get a good answer from the Rabbi, but at least it gives him a chance to sound off and possibly vent his feelings.

###

Saun enters Rob's office. "Hey, guy, I got the info you ask me to try and get. The main office of the Yard contacted the Mossad again and after much pressure was able to get them to share some intel with us. It turns out they have been able to identify one of the murdered men. He was an SS guard, and he is or was on the war crimes criminal list. The guy called George Caraway was in reality August Schroder. They were even able to locate where he was stationed. He was a guard at Dachau Prison."

"This is great news," says Rob. "Finally, a lead and something to go on. I bet if we look real hard, we should be able to find a list of Germans who were guards at Dachau. If we can find that list, then we might be able to compare it to other names."

Saun says, "That, is a good idea, but remember, the guards have all taken false names, so we will need to find at least one more original name. If we are to pinpoint who was where and when, that information should lead us to a list of who was working where in the prison, and, if lucky, we might find that the list of names is from a particular prison section, hopefully. Once we have that list, then we can get an idea about who else might be on the killer's hit list."

"I agree with you Rob, but how are we going to cross-reference those names to the new fake names taken by the guards today?"

"Good question, Saun. Wish I had a good answer for you. All I can say is, let's take it one step at a time and see where it takes us.'

"What else can we do?"

Sometime later, Rob and Saun are having coffee and just generally killing time with small talk.

They are in Rob's office, and Rob has his feet up on the corner of his desk when he asks Saun, "Say, guy, how long you been at this, this chasing bad guys?"

"I think about twenty years here pretty soon, old boy. As a matter of fact, I was considering retiring. I thought, if I retire early, I can get another job, and with my retirement money and the new job, then my wife and I might finally be able to live comfortably. Then the wildest thing happened. One day, my wife gets a ring on the door buzzer and when she opens the door, this American guy, a lawyer type, is standing there with an attaché case. He introduces himself and says that he was there on behalf of her deceased father, Solomon Berkowitz. That was my wife's maiden name—Berkowitz. It seems that Solomon had become friends in Dachau Prison with another Jewish prisoner who was quite wealthy.

Well, it seems that, in his will, this guy wanted to take care of any of his friends' surviving family members. So he gives her this attaché case and when she opens it, it has two million pounds in it! He tells her it belongs to her and is tax free. He is not at liberty to tell her who his client is or where the money came from. When this happened, I didn't see or feel the need to retire so soon. What was I going to do with my life, if I retired? You know, Rob, it is really strange how life deals out the cards. If another weird incident had not happened, then we would not have gotten all that money.

Rob asks him, "What might that have been?"

"Well, you see, my wife at the time of the war was just a child imprisoned at Dachau Prison. She was about seven or eight years old at the time. Her mother had already been killed by the Nazis. She and a large group of small children—she thinks the number had to be in excess of 100 small children— they had been stripped naked, put in line, and told they were about to take a shower. Well, while in line to go into the shower, the American Army entered the camp and liberated every one of them. We put two and two together and figured out the Nazis were not lining the children up for a shower. They were going to kill them by gas. The shower was a gas chamber."

Rob looked at Saun. "That is an incredible story."

"So, because of that, and two million pounds, I am able to be here today, enjoying your wonderful company."

Both had a good laugh over that statement.

After a few days of searching, Scotland Yard has some success. Saun tells Rob, "Scotland Yard has found the list of German guards at Dachau Prison. They are sending it to us via the wire."

Within an hour, the two inspectors are going over the Dachau Prison guards list of names. They are comparing it to the list of names on the war crimes personnel list.

"Okay, here is the one name we already know of. Here is George Caraway alias August Schroder. Schroder was stationed at section four of the prison. We need to go back and find at least one more name of a guard—his original name—then we can cross it over to our list and hopefully find that both worked in the same section. From there, we will have a working list of names," says Saun

Rob says, "For the sake of time and travel, let's start with the closet name and see if we can get lucky."

"That would be Al Miller, who was murdered in Chicago. As a matter of fact, he was the first one killed."

"Okay, we are off to Chicago."

Saun and Rob grab a plane and head for Chicago. Upon arrival, they have the local FBI branch agent Richard Merrywither pick them up and escort them to their office.

Merrywither is introducing himself and his assistant when he says, "Please call me Dick. I am the chief agent in Chicago, and we will help all we can."

"Fine, Dick. What I need you to do is send as many people as you can out to the neighborhood of the first victim, Al Miller. Nose around the community and find out as much about him as you can. See if he left any clues as to his early life, where he may have been from or where he was during the war years. We also need to contact the local police and get a set of fingerprints of the victim. I am sure they have them on file from the autopsy.

"Then I want you to contact Central Identification and see if we can get a match on the prints," says Rob.

"Gotcha, Inspector. We'll get our people on it immediately."

By mid-afternoon, the guys in the field didn't have much to add that Saun and Rob didn't already know. They did have the prints, however, which were already being scanned for a match.

Two hours later, Saun tells Rob that he has some good news. "Interpol has a match on the finger prints. It seems they belong to an Albert Muller, formally of Brackenheim, Germany, who, before the war, was a night guard for a short time at a German bank." Rob looks at the guys and adds, "Apparently, our man was not too creative in trying to hide his identity. He went from Albert Muller to Al Miller."

Immediately the men start to crosscheck the names of the Dachau Prison guards, and soon Rob says, "Bingo, we have another hit. This is our lucky day—section 4 again. The only two names we have, and they both were guards at section 4. I will bet that the list of people being killed is a list of SS officers from section 4 of Dachau." Rob then adds, "We may crack this case yet."

Saun comments, "Now all we need to do is narrow the guard list down to only those who were stationed at section 4."

They sit down at a table and crosscheck name after name until they have a list of their own. Upon doing this, the inspectors create a list of thirty-five men which they then crosscheck against the war crimes list, whittling it down to a solid eighteen.

Saun says, "Of this list of eighteen, we need to run a check to see how many are still alive and whether Geneva has records on any of them."

Saun picks up the phone and contacts Scotland Yard home office again. He gives his boss the information needed and asks him to expedite it, if he can.

Rob turns to Merrywither. "I think we are done here in Chicago, Agent Merrywither. I want to thank you. You and your men have been a big help."

The guys leave and head back to the airport.

Back at Rob's office, the two inspectors dive deep into trying to make heads or tails out of the names on the list in order to see if anything jumps out at them. After several days, Scotland Yard calls Saun and tells him they are wiring him the list of names they have been able to pull out of the files that might have any relevance or validity at all.

When the list comes through, Saun, Rob and several of their assistants realize that they now have a list of about eleven names. These are war-crime criminals who no one knows anything about but are presumed to be still alive and in hiding. The two investigators spend some more time cross-referencing names.

Rob finally says, "Gentlemen, after checking the lists we have, I think we can safely say that we have narrowed it down to five men. Here is the list. Falco Berger. Conrad Kaiser. Emmerich Kruger. Emil Hohler. Franz Heinrich.

"Now, all we have to do is figure out where each of these men is. Gentlemen, that is going to be as hard a job as the rest of the case has been up 'til now. However, I have a plan. It might take some time, but I am hopeful it might work and at the very least, help us to narrow the list down some more.

"Let me propose a question to you. If you were on the run, but you had family like a mother or father or others still back in your original hometown, is it not reasonable to assume that, sooner or later, you would make contact with them? I am going to have the home office pull these men's records and find out where they grew up, where their parents might be. We then will put undercover agents in each hometown, infiltrate them as deeply as we can. A little nosing around just might reap some reward. If we get lucky again, we may find out where they are, or at least the name they are living under. Remember, it has been twenty-five years now, so they have to have developed some feeling of safety by now."

"Good idea, Saun. Just think, when Scotland Yard sent you over here, they said you were just another pretty face."

"Yeah, yeah."

###

David finds himself fighting the demons that pursue him night after night. David was never the most religious of men, but he did have a certain feeling of religion that most warriors have. Having been a Navy SEAL, he knows that all warriors have this feeling of right and might on their side, and along with this comes the knowledge that you will prevail. He knows what he is doing is not legal, and that, if caught, he will be treated as just another mass murderer, in spite of what public opinion seems to be. But he decides he must continue to do his father's work.

A trip to Miami Florida is planned, and one of the names on the list just happens to be in Miami, so David starts to make preparations for both the business trip and the event.

He tells his wife, "I will be gone for a few days, and when I get back, I will cook dinner for you the likes of which you have never seen."

Loraine looks at him and says, "Since when do you know how to cook?"

"Never you mind, woman. I can do anything I set my mind to."

With this, he gives all the kisses and hugs again, and he is off.

He gets into Miami late in the evening and decides to check out the home address of the next victim, James Kinkade. South Harbor is where he heads after getting the rental. After following Kinkade, David learns that he turns out to be the owner of a small store.

He often seems to work late, and he is not in a heavily trafficked area. It seems like this one is almost falling in place for David. He stalks Kinkade, who is rather small in stature, and gets a good feel for his habits and what goes on around his store. It is a kind of feed and farm supply, so to get a better feel for the store, he walks in to buy something.

As he is walking around, Kinkade asks, "Can I help you?"

David says, "I am just browsing for now, but I have some pests that are getting in my barn. What would you recommend to get rid of them?"

Kinkade walks over to him, reaches up on the shelf, and pulls down a bottle of poison. "This is pretty powerful stuff, so you want to keep it away from any people."

David asks, "Well, how powerful is it?"

"Let me put it this way, sir. If a human swallowed it, they would have about three minutes of life left. You don't play games with this stuff. Quite frankly, it has been banned by the government, so once I sell this batch, there won't be any more."

David counters with, "That's really interesting. I surely wouldn't want to have anyone I know swallow it." Then he leaves.

That evening, as David sits outside the store in the parking lot across the street, he watches Kinkade get ready to close the store. Then he makes his move, crosses the street, and enters the store.

Kinkade yells, "We are just closing." Then he recognizes the man from earlier and asks, "Well, did you decide upon the poison?"

David answers, "Sure did, and no one I know is going to take it."

"Wise move, mister. Wise move," says Kinkade.

David pulls out his 9mm pistol and lets Kinkade see it.

Kinkade says, "Not another robbery. Why won't you people leave me alone? I have been robbed four times in two years."

David says, "I can assure you, you won't have any more robberies. Let me ask you a question. What is your name, the one you used at Dachau?"

Upon hearing this, Kinkade knows this is the man in the news, the one they call the "Revengeful Murderer," and he sprints for the back door, but David is much too big and fast for him.

"Tell me, Falco Berger, SS guard, did you feel anything for the people you killed at Dachau? I can assure you, I will not feel anything for you as you drink this bottle of poison." David holds up the bottle of poison.

Kinkade pleads for his life, and certainly does not want to be subjected to the kind of death that he has just been told he will be forced to endure. With that, David grabs him. Kinkade tries feverishly to fight David, but David is just too big. As Kinkade screams and yells, his mouth is open. David pours the poison in.

Just like the man said, two or three minutes is all it takes.

David looks at Kinkade and says; "At least you're a man of your word. Three minutes exactly."

David finishes the job by leaving his calling card in Kinkade's forehead.

###

The next day, the newspapers are having a field day with this new murder by the "Revengeful Murderer." Pictures abound, with Kinkade lying on the floor and some kind of foam pouring out of his mouth, the poison bottle on the ground next to him. The headlines read" *Another Nazi War Criminal Found Dead, Work of the "Revengeful Murderer."*

Rob gets the information off the wire and instantly sends an agent to Miami to find out as much as he can. Most important, to find out the dead man's original name.

Again, David returns home from his business trip, just as he has done hundreds of times, and as usual, Loraine asks, "Did you have a successful trip?"

"You know, dear, I really didn't care much for this guy. I thought he was little mouthy about the whole thing. I had a hard time getting him to digest the idea I was putting forth, but we were still able to bring an end to the negotiations."

Back at the FBI office, the guys are discussing the case. Saun looks at Rob and says, "Well, that brings the list to four."

"You do realize, Rob, if we take much longer, we won't need to catch the guy. The killings will be over. I tell you, Rob, I'm beginning to wonder what it will be like if we *do* catch him. I get the feeling it will be almost like catching Robin Hood. With the lawyers you have in this country, they will get him off as justifiable homicide."

A few days later, the FBI agent sent to Miami has returned and has the name they wanted. The agent says, "His alias was James Kinkade, but his real name was Falco Berger, and he was originally from Leutenberg, Germany."

"Good work. Well done. For that I am going to splurge and buy you a cup of coffee," says Rob.

"Gee, boss, will I have to declare this on my income tax return?"

The guys pull out their list and sure enough there is Berger, and he was stationed at—you guessed it—section four.

CHAPTER 11

"Well, we are down to four names, but we still have no idea where these men are," Rob tells Saun. "If we knew that, we could put a tail on each and maybe catch this guy."

"You know, Rob, I can't help but feel something is going to break for us reasonably soon," says Saun.

###

David looks at his own copy of the list of names and realizes that he is down to only two remaining. He feels a sense of urgency to complete the job and tell his father, "I have done what you ask." At the same time, he senses the relief that is waiting for him once the deed has been completed.

David heads for Cleveland and the next to last job. The plane ride from San Diego to Cleveland Hopkins International airport, with stops and time changes, is about six hours and fifty-five minutes, so David plans to arrive in the late afternoon. He does his ritual car rental and then heads for the hotel. He has shipped his tranquilizing dart gun ahead to his hotel via UPS.

When David travels, he makes a Xerox copy of the list of names that he'd taken from his father's original diary. He does not want to take a chance on losing something so valuable to him as his father's diary. It is the only thing he has of his father's, and it is extremely important to him.

When David checks into the hotel, he asks for the package that was pre-shipped to him. The clerk finds it and hands it to him. David tips the clerk and leaves.

David does all the necessary preliminary detail work including checking out the house and the surrounding area just to make sure nothing is out of the ordinary that could cause him a problem. Finally, he checks his pocket to make sure he has the mask he always wears, so that if anyone sees him, they could not identify him.

The house is big and old. It seems to have lights on only in one particular room, on the first floor in the front. As David cases the house, he can see that this is the living room and the TV is playing. There appears to be only one person in the house, so David begins his approach to the house. He jimmies the back door, which opens extremely easy. David thinks that this man could use a security alarm system. He can't help himself from thinking the lack of one is going to be the death of this man.

Once he is in the house, he works his way toward the living room where he hears voices. At first, he is startled, thinking that there is maybe more than one person in the house. Then he remembers the TV and is convinced that the voices are from a television program.

As he makes his way closer to the living room, he becomes excited at the thought of finishing the job. Just then, his coat pocket gets caught on a very small nail that is sticking out of the door frame on the open door that leads. David is forced into the nail and then jerks back. After making sure nothing is wrong, he continues on with his hunt for the victim.

As David is just about to lunge out into view of the target, someone walks into the hall, turns the corner, and is standing there, staring at David. With reflexes like a fox, David fires the dart gun in his left hand, and the man drops to the floor.

With this obstacle out of the way, David continues with the killing of his target subject and leaves the ritual Star of David on his forehead. This time, however, David deviates just slightly from his original format. He leaves a small typed note on the victim.

The note simply says:

One more to go. My father will be proud of me.

David leaves satisfied he has done his usual efficient job. As he goes, though, he is a bit fearful about the unintended person whom he had to dart. Since he has no way of knowing this person's physical condition, he fears the man might die from the drugs in the dart. So David decides to call the local police and tell them the house number where they will find two men, one dead and the other passed out. That way, he figures, if the guy is allergic to the drugs, at least he won't die since first aid will be on the way.

###

Rob and Saun are looking at the wire service when they see that he has struck again. Realizing that the FBI and Scotland Yard have been tracking this case, the local Cleveland police department, once done with their local forensic checks, informs them all about the note they found at the crime scene. The two inspectors are told about the murder as well, and that the note stated *"One more to go."*

Quickly they pull out their list and examine it to try and figure out who might be the last candidate. Again they swiftly send a representative to Cleveland, to see if they can get an original identity for the victim and attempt to scratch off another name on the list. Their hope is still to figure out who the murderer's final victim is going to be.

Agent Garry Sonders is sent to Cleveland, hoping for some more luck on gathering information. After arriving in Cleveland, Agent Sonders introduces himself and asks to see the crime scene. It is still blocked off with police tape but with permission he very meticulously looks the scene over, trying to make sure he doesn't miss anything.

As he is moving about the house, he walks past the cellar door and his suit coat comes in contact with a small nail sticking out of the door molding. This is the same nail that David got caught on during the killing.

Upon feeling the nail, Garry jumps back and discovers it has put a very slight tear in his very best jacket. After a few choice words appropriate for just such an occasion, he looks at the nail.

He gets pissed at this nail and decides to show it who is boss. "I will fix you, nail," says Garry as he takes his shoe off and starts to tap it back in place.

For some stupid reason, it is easier to stand and hit the nail if the door is open, so he opens the door and as he positions his body to strike the nail, something catches his eye. Lying right there, on the top step of the cellar steps, is a folded piece of paper.

Agent Sonders reaches down and picks it up then unfolds it and starts to read it. In about fifteen seconds, he realizes what he has in his hands. He puts the paper back in his pocket and says nothing to anyone. He wants to get back to the office with the piece of paper, but he has another job to finish first, the one he was sent there to do.

It takes Garry about six hours to finally track down the victim's real name, so it is then he busts his ass back to Washington with the new evidence he has found. As he finally bursts into the office, excited as hell, the guys are all over him, trying to calm him down. He pulls out the piece of paper and hands it to his boss, Rob. As Rob starts to study it, his whole face lights up like a Christmas tree.

"This is it. This is it! This is the break we have spent months looking for." He looks skyward and says, "Thank you, God." Then he passes the note to Saun.

It only takes a moment for Saun to start going bananas, as well. Apparently, the list that David took with him to the murder was in his coat pocket. When he bumped into the nail in the house, it caught the paper and pulled it from his pocket, tossing it down the steps. When someone closed the basement door, it was hidden from view. But Garry opened the door to hit the nail and was able to discover it still lying there.

The guys quickly take out their own master list out. The last guy killed, in Cleveland, was Stephen Walters. His original name was Franz Heinrich and he was an SS guard. As they study David's list they now know: Conrad Kaiser of Lapseville, New York is the intended last victim.

"Now that we know who the last victim is going to be and even where he lives, all we have to do is put a stake out on him, and when our killer shows up, we nab him."

"Elementary, Doctor Watson," says Saun. "Elementary."

Both men grin from ear to ear, realizing they are about to catch the Revengeful Murderer.

The German SS captain of the guards at Dachau, Conrad Kaiser, is well aware of the "Revengeful Murderer and the killings that have been taking place. He is a basket case about now.

He knows he is on the list and that his number is very close, so he is very skittish and nervous of everyone and everything. He has taken to carrying a gun and rarely talks to people he doesn't know.

After the Cleveland revelation, the two inspectors have had their agents identify Conrad in

New York and locate him. They go to his town and set up a surveillance team to keep track of Kaiser, beginning to track him and make a list of his habits so they have some idea what to expect, should he get spooked.

Kaiser is a rather big man with the personality of a snake. He doesn't come out too often, but when he does, it is for his traditional walk down the street to get his coffee and donuts.

The team is on the job but it soon becomes pretty boring, sitting there doing nothing except watch Kaiser's apartment.

When David copied his father's list from the diary, he was very fortunate: he did not copy the entire letter, just the names. If he had copied the entire list, his father's name would have been on it, and the trail back to David would have been an easy one to follow. Since it was just a partial list, connecting David to the list at this time is still impossible. What that means is that the FBI still doesn't know who they are looking for or what the Revengeful Murdered looks like. They agree that he still could be anybody, so with this in mind, anyone who shows up on the street is very carefully scrutinized.

David has realized that he lost the list, so he has no choice but to assume it was lost at the last crime scene. He is certain that the law, surely, has figured out what the list means and who still remains alive— that is to say, who is the last victim. This is going to make things difficult for David: he can no longer come and go as freely as he has in the past.

He gives a lot of thought to this new twist and seriously toys with the idea of calling it quits. One more victim surely won't make any difference, he reasons, and the risk is great at this stage of the game. The problem with this idea, however, is that the last name on the list was purposely designed to be the last name because he was known as The Butcher. He was the worst of the worst. If any man deserved to die, it *had* to be the Butcher.

So David convinces himself that he must finish what he has started. No one else is going to give this man the justice he deserves, so it has to be him.

CHAPTER 12

David has another business trip coming up
pretty soon in New York City, so he intends to
fabricate some reason for staying over a few extra
days. This will give him time to case the area where
his final victim resides in order to watch both the
target, Kaiser, as well as the police who have to be
surveilling him.

He makes his family aware that he will be
traveling to New York and back within the week.
Then he catches a plane to New York City and, once
there, sets about instigating his plan. This time it is
going to take a good bit of preparation and planning
to pull off his hit without getting caught.

This idea of getting caught begins to play heavily
on David's mind. In the past, things have gone like
clockwork. But now, the police know who his
intended target is and even where he lives, so anyone
trying to get to him has to be suspect.

Once in New York, David rents an SUV and
heads north to upstate New York and a small town

known as Lapseville. It has only about twenty-eight thousand people and closely resembles of the town featured in the TV show *Mayberry RFD* that starred Andy Griffin.

The town's small size will work to David's advantage, because it will be difficult for an out-of-towner to hide around there; any strangers will stick out like a sore thumb, which should make spotting the FBI agents easy.

David checks into the local hotel and then spends the rest of the day buying supplies and trolling around town, getting used to what is what and where everything is. It isn't long before David is able to spot his target, Conrad Kaiser. He watches Kaiser for several hours as he goes about his tasks, doing those things people do to exist in a small town like grocery shopping, paying bills, and so on. One thing David takes special notice of is the fact that Kaiser likes to take a late-afternoon walk about 4:00 PM.

Kaiser always leaves his downtown apartment, goes west on Saymore Street for four blocks, passes the local appliance store on the corner, then goes around the block and heads east for a few more blocks until he comes to the local coffee shop. He sits there on a sidewalk chair for about twenty minutes, enjoys his coffee and a donut, then heads back home.

As David watches Kaiser, he is interested in watching the law enforcement guys who trail him every step of the way. The FBI men don't get too close, since the town is so small, but if need be, they can be on the spot in no time flat. They stay back about half a block, and they certainly do not move very fast.

Of particular interest to David is how long Kaiser is out of their sight when he turns the corner next to the appliance store. It must take the agents two to three minutes before they turn the same corner. One would think they would have other agents posted around the town, so as to be able to pick him up as they pass him off from one agent to another. But they don't. Again, this is likely due to the small size of the town.

After spending a couple days tracking the target and learning what his regular habits are, David starts the second phase of his plan.

He goes into the appliance store and tells the owner, "I am a marketing and advertising agent from New York, and I have been looking for a store just like this in a town just this size for almost a year now to shoot some advertising training films for one of my big clients." He asks the owner, "Would you consider renting the store to me for, say, forty-eight hours, so I can finally get my job done before my boss fires me? Would you consider renting it for, say, $50,000 for the two days?"

The owner hears fifty thousand dollars and says, "For that, you can have it for the month!"

"Nah, my boss says I have to be back at the office by the day after tomorrow. Forty-eight hours will be plenty."

"When do you want it?"

"How about after 5:00 today?" David asks.

"No problem."

"By the way, I would like you to show me how to turn the lights on and off and how to lock up. If I am going to take responsibility for your store, I want to make sure I lock up right. I don't want anything to happen that is going to cost me more money."

At 5:00 that afternoon, David stops by the store, and the owner is very impressed with David and his desire to be responsible. So much so, he practically throws the keys at him so he can head out of town.

As he gets in his car to leave, he tells David, "I am finally going to get in a couple days of fishing."

After taking the keys and waving goodbye to the store owner, David locks the door to the store and heads for the town about twenty-five miles down the road. Upon arrival, he goes to the largest appliance store he can find.

There, he goes in and asks a sales clerk, "I am interested in buying five of the largest refrigerators you have and four of your electric dryers." He also tells him, "I will need them delivered to Lapseville by 9:00 AM tomorrow morning. As a matter of fact, if you give me your word that they will be there, I will give you $500 as a tip."

The clerk's eyes light up, hearing about a five-hundred-dollar tip. He says, "Just a minute. Let me check with the owner and make sure we can meet your demands." After three minutes, he comes back with a big smile on his face and says, "No problem."

"Good," says David. "Now, I want you to deliver them to the appliance store on Saymore Street and East Second Avenue. If no one is there to greet you, then all you need to do is stack the items on the sidewalk outside the store, and I will have my employees take them inside when we open.

"Not a problem. You can count on us," says the clerk.

"I'm sure I can. How about you getting me a receipt? I want to pay you cash for this sale."

The clerk leaves and in a few minutes returns with the bill. David pulls out his utility bag and, with a handful of money, pays the young man.

David asks, "Now, where is the closest hardware store?"

"That's easy. Just four doors down the street. That would be Becket's Hardware."

David shakes his hand and says, "Thank you. You have been a big help."

Then he heads for the hardware store where he meets the clerk and says, "I need a cordless 3/8 drill, an assortment of screws and washers, then a piece of half-plywood, about a two foot by two foot square section. Next, I need a handful of heavy duty construction spikes and a hammer. By the way, I need a good two-inch-wide metal chisel, as well." Then he asks the clerk, "Do you have any wide, heavy-duty Velcro?"

"Sure do. Right over there next to the lawn chair weaving stuff."

"That will work. I will need about fifteen feet of it. I also need some heavy rope. That should do it." David pays for everything, puts the goods in his SUV, and heads back to Lapseville.

He pulls up to the store, unlocks it, and then goes inside, taking in with him all the supplies he's just bought. Next, he begins to case the interior of the building to get an understanding of where everything is. There is a back room with a nice, relatively new, thick wood table. "Ah-ha! This will work nicely," he says to himself.

David has brought with him his air pistol that fires darts like those used to tranquilize animals in the zoo. He takes the gun out of its box and lays it on the table, setting its CO-2 cartridges next to it.

Then he takes out a small vial of clear fluid. This fluid is designed to put large animals to sleep and to do it fast. David was told when he bought it, "If you use it on a human, they will be out like a light before they can take a single step." The guy also said, "And it will keep them out for at least six to eight hours."

David is pleased with him work for the day and is certain the plan will work. All he has to do is make sure he does exactly what is planned within the time frame he has allowed. Any deviation from this by as little as thirty seconds, however, and it might mean the end for David. All that is needed now is a good night's sleep.

That is easier said than done. David knows that this is the climax, the end of the chase, the last name on the list. If he can pull this off then he is home free. It will be the last of the killing, and David's life can return to normal. But if he fails, then he could wind up in the electric chair, paying with his own life.

Early the next morning, about 7:00 AM, David starts to put things in motion. He gets dressed and checks the old, used clothing he has brought with him. He also checks the tin cup and stack of pencils he packed. Then he pulls out the little ragged sign he made that hangs around his neck and says, *Buy a pencil, Help the poor.* Once his panhandler costume is complete and everything is in order, off to the store David heads.

The first thing he does is fasten the plywood to the bottom of a wood chair, so the hand truck will grab hold of it. Then he takes the Velcro and cuts it into strips about four feet long and then screws them with washers to the sides of the chair. Now the chair has restraining straps attached to it, one set of straps for each arm and a set for the legs.

By mid-morning, the refrigerators he bought the day before have arrived and are setting alongside the building, just as most businesses do when bringing in new inventory. He takes a hand truck and brings one of the refrigerators inside the store. David then cuts the bottom of the box and lifts it off the refrigerator. Next, he takes the empty box back outside and sets it next to the others so it looks as if it is still part of the new inventory, as well. But the box is really hiding the chair with the Velcro. This also makes it difficult for anyone to see him.

The day moves on, and David's moment of truth is coming fast. In another half hour, it will be action time. David begins to get excited, even more than normal.

He dresses in his old clothes designed to make him look like a panhandler. He adds an old wig and mustache, as well as some broken sunglasses. He grabs his tin cup with the pencils, puts the sign around his neck, and then goes outside. He takes the refrigerator box off the chair momentarily, partially exposing the chair.

As he is standing on the corner, doing his panhandling, he can see the target is only one store away from him. David also sees the FBI agents following at their traditional distance, half a block back.

David takes out his air dart pistol, which has been loaded and made ready for the shot. Just as Kaiser turns the corner, David shoves the tin cup in his face and asks him to buy a pencil, at the same time taking the dart gun and shooting Kaiser. Kaiser goes limp almost instantly, whereupon David shoves him into the chair.

But then something happens that was not planned. Kaiser slips out of David's hands and starts to slide to the ground. Valuable time is being lost, and he knows it. This is exactly the kind of thing that David knew could kill his attempt.

He responds as quickly as he can, realizing he is using up valuable seconds, and seconds are all he has. All he can do is pick Kaiser back up and set him in the chair while trying to hurry, as originally planned, and hope the FBI agents don't turn the corner before he has a chance to hide Kaiser under the box.

By now, David is beginning to shake. Valuable time has been lost. *Will he make it?* David's heart is pounding so loud and fast, he is sure he is about to get caught.

He flips the Velcro straps around Kaiser so he can't slide out again, and then picks up the empty refrigerator box, hurriedly setting it over top of Kaiser before swiftly going back to being a panhandler again. Just as David stands up straight, the FBI agents turn the corner, and they actually bump into him, knocking the cup and pencils out of his hand.

David, without missing a beat, yells at them and says, "Hey, man, what the hell ya doin'? This is my livin' you knocking all over the street."

The agents apologize and help him pick up the pencils. It is then that they realize: Kaiser is nowhere to be seen.

One of the agents asks the panhandler, "Did you see a heavy set old man go past here?"

"Yea man. Like a big dude? He went that a-way."
And he points down the road."

The agents start to run like crazy to catch up to the man.

At this time, David slips into the store, brings out the hand truck he had set just inside the door, picks up the refrigerator box that has Kaiser strapped to the chair, and takes him into the store's back room. David then hangs a sign on the front of the store that says, *Closed. Gone home for an emergency.*

By this time, the FBI agents are going crazy trying to find Kaiser. They even double back and check the boxes alongside the store to make sure they really have inventory in them. Then the FBI has no idea what to do. They cannot locate him anywhere. The FBI agents go crazy, turning the town upside down looking for Kaiser, but he is nowhere to be found.

Later that evening, about 8:30 PM, Kaiser starts to wake up, and the minute he does, he realizes he is in deep trouble. He is tied to a chair facing a table. Both of his hands are stretched out and lying palms face down on the table, and he has a gag in his mouth.

What he then realizes is that his hands are face down on the table because they have been nailed to the table with big, heavy-duty construction spikes. By this time, he is also realizing the pain that goes along with the spikes in his hands. He then notices that lying on the table is a metal cutting chisel and a hammer.

###

In a couple of days, the FBI receives a phone call from the local police in Lapseville.

"We have found the guy you were looking for who came up missing. You need to see this to believe it."

That afternoon, Rob and Saun are standing in the appliance store on Saymore Street. In the backroom, there, sitting in a chair, is Conrad Kaiser, blood all over the place. Ten little fingers lie on the table next to a chisel and hammer. His forehead has the Star of David cut into it.

Pinned to his shirt is a note that reads as follows:

It's over, the voices of Dachau can sleep now, my father would have been proud of me.

Rob turns to Saun and says, "Well, I guess that is the end of that. I really thought we would catch him before this, but in a way I am kinda glad we didn't.

Those SOBs got what they deserved, even if it wasn't through the normal justice system."

Saun gets a kind of funny look on his face and says to Rob, "I have to agree with you, as much as it irks me to not close the case. You know, Rob, I sure would like to have met this guy. It is intriguing to wonder what kind of person he must be.

"Well, I guess I am off to England—but you know, I think I will hang it up now. This chasing bad guys all over the globe is getting old. Speaking of meeting someone, I sure would like to have met the guy who gave my wife the two million pounds—just to say thanks. With my wife's inheritance, I really don't need this anymore. Sitting on my boat, fishing and drinking a cold beer, sounds awfully good to me about now."

###

Six months pass. David is home again. He, along with his family and a few of his best friends are relaxing on the boat and having a great time.

David walks to the rear of the boat, holds up his beer bottle as if making a toast, and points to the sky. "To you," he says. "I did what you asked."

Loraine yells at him, "What are you doing?"

David answers, "Just making a toast to a dear, close friend. Someone I knew but never had the chance to get to know well."

THE END

Please feel free to write a review of this book
or any of my books and send it to
mbblair@aol.com
For information about my other books, visit
www.williamblairbooks.com

ABOUT THE AUTHOR

Hello out there to my new friends. Thank you for taking time to read my book. I sincerely hope that you enjoyed it. What should I say about myself?

This is the last of ten books I have written. The first is *WSTA: Winning Social Tennis for Seniors*, a great guide to enjoying and improving your tennis game. I have also written *The Execution of Dreams* for entrepreneurs and small-business owners; and *Chasing God,* about what we think about when we refer to God, full of questions of the heart. I also just published the first of a series of books with humorous essays called *Incidence of Stupidity,* and two action thrillers, *The Stratton Formula* and *The Omega Department and the UFO.* I have three other novels finished that I hope to make available in the very near future.

I am a small-(but not too small)-town boy from Wheeling, West Virginia (pop. 35,000), which is about fifty miles south of Pittsburg, Pennsylvania.

People are surprised when they hear us talk. They expect to hear a lot of "y'all's." Well, we are just far enough north of the Mason-Dixon Line that, instead of "y'all," we say "you'se guys" and call a creek a "crik." Also, we don't wash our cars: we "warsh" them. Get the point?

I may not be the smartest bear in town, but I was able to grub out a pretty decent living. I am the son of Reece Blair, a policeman in Wheeling for twenty-two years and then the Sheriff of our county for eight. Honesty was a pretty strong thing in our family. Except for an incident which I mention in my first book, *The Execution of Dreams,* that occurred when I was about seven or eight, I pretty much lived by Dad's rules.

I had normal high school years, playing football and baseball. (My girlfriend wouldn't let me play basketball.) I graduated along with the rest of my friends... Well, not really...

I think they may have thrown me out... Or maybe I snuck out the back door. You see, in high school I majored in sports, cars, and girls—not necessarily in that order. For those of you who are car buffs, I had a 1941 Hollywood Graham supercharged six-cylinder which I customized during my sophomore year.

I got out of high school and started college at West Liberty State College. I took test after test at first and didn't pass a one, so I decided that college wasn't for me. Some years later I discovered that no one else was passing those tests, either: they were designed to weed out those who really wanted a college education. Well, it worked.

I left college and joined the U.S. Air Force in 1958. There, I found my calling as a jet airplane mechanic. All those years working with my dad began to pay off—my dad was a really remarkable man.

After I spent four years in the USAF, my enlistment was up so my father and I decided to start an Automobile Radiator Repair Garage. Dad and I were off and flying in the repair business. There I was: *in business.* Dad let me run things, even when I was wrong. He let me make my mistakes and boy, did I make a bunch. Then, Dad stepped back, looked me square in the eye and said, "I told you so."

But on the other hand, when I succeeded he put his fingers in his suspenders, pulled them out proudly, puffed his chest and said, "Look at my son, the Doctor."

It wasn't long before I was off and running in all kinds of directions. I lived by the theory that you should throw a bunch of fishing poles in the water, and then eat the biggest fish we caught.

The next addition to our cause was the Automobile Air Conditioning Business." We did well. In fact, I was the first radiator shop in the country to be nationally certified as a heating *and* cooling expert.

It wasn't too long before a series of other businesses crossed my path. I started a Gravely Tractor Agency and, later, a small excavation company that specialized in miniature equipment designed to get into spaces that big equipment could not.

I came within the eleventh hour of a deal to bring an aircraft manufacturing company to our city, which was neat because, by this time, I had gotten my pilot's license. Not too long after that I introduced "ultrasonic sound" to the radiator industry for cleaning radiators; it is still used around the world today. Then, my Oil Cooler business took root and became our biggie. This is what led me to receive recognition as *1991 Entrepreneur of the Year* in West Virginia.

For some reason, I found myself drawn toward politics. Why? I wish I knew. Was it ego? Or did I really want to help the small business people in our state, as I told everyone? I was doing pretty well in the political race for governor of West Virginia when my business caught on fire, and I had to withdraw from the race in order to rebuild it. Soon thereafter, my two sons came into the business and eventually took over. The rest is history.

I don't think I did too badly in life! Along with my wife, I introduced four super great children into the world. (Did you notice how I didn't take *all* the credit for the children?) I then started several businesses, and gave jobs and opportunities to a whole lot of young people who wanted to enter the business world. I developed a new technology for an industry that is still being used today, and received several patents on some unique items that we still manufacture to this day.

Of my four children, the two girls and their two children—we love and miss deeply, as they are living out of town, but I did succeed in bringing two of my four children to our home town, where my wife and I enjoy the six grandchildren. I have a nice home, a beautiful wife, and a pretty kitty that sleeps under my armpit every night.

By the way, about four years ago, at age seventy, I became nationally certified as a professional tennis coach. I play tennis four days a week and teach tennis five times a week.

I have all this and a couple cold beers in the refrigerator:

What more can a person ask for?!

#####

You can contact me here:
mbblair@aol.com
www.williamblairbooks.com

Made in the USA
Middletown, DE
28 October 2022

13673719R00091